"Thanks for the update, Sheriff," Nick said. He reached over and took the doll from the bench. **"We found this on the flagpole this morning."**

The sheriff examined the doll for a moment before shaking his head. "Someone's definitely trying to send you a message."

Nick placed his hand on Molly's back, wanting her to know that he was there to support her. "We've gotten the message loud and clear."

The sheriff raised an eyebrow. "You're not going to take heed of the warning, I take it?"

Molly shook her head. "I'm staying right here."

Finally, the sheriff nodded and took a step back toward his sedan. "So be it, then. Do be careful. I don't want these incidents to escalate."

"Neither do we," Nick assured him.

Molly wrapped her arms over her chest and looked into the distance as the sheriff pulled away.

More than anything Nick wanted to protect Molly—both her heart and her physical well-being. But he wasn't sure which would be harder.

Books by Christy Barritt

Love Inspired Suspense

Keeping Guard
The Last Target
Race Against Time
Ricochet

CHRISTY BARRITT

loves stories and has been writing them for as long as she can remember. She gets her best ideas when she's supposed to be paying attention to something else—like in a workshop or while driving down the road.

The second book in her Squeaky Clean Mystery series, *Suspicious Minds,* won the inspirational category of the 2009 Daphne du Maurier Award for Excellence in Suspense and Mystery. She's also the coauthor of *Changed: True Stories of Finding God in Christian Music.*

When she's not working on books, Christy writes articles for various publications. She's also a weekly feature writer for the *Virginian-Pilot* newspaper, the worship leader at her church and a frequent speaker at various writers' groups, women's luncheons and church events.

She's married to Scott, a teacher and funny man extraordinaire. They have two sons, two dogs and a houseplant named Martha.

To learn more about her, visit her website, www.christybarritt.com.

RICOCHET

Christy Barritt

Love Inspired

Recycling programs
for this product may
not exist in your area.

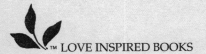

™ LOVE INSPIRED BOOKS

ISBN-13: 978-0-373-44507-3

RICOCHET

Copyright © 2012 by Christy Barritt

www.LoveInspiredBooks.com

Printed in U.S.A.

The voice of the Lord twists the oaks and strips the forests bare. And in his temple all cry, Glory!
—*Psalms* 29:9

This book is dedicated to Camp Rudolph,
a place filled with memories of sweet friendships,
skinned knees, the dreaded bat game
and powerful God encounters.

ONE

*T*hump!

Molly Hamilton's sedan rose and then sank back to the ground as if she'd gone over a speed bump. A really large speed bump.

As she threw on the brakes, every muscle in her body tensed. She gripped the steering wheel, frozen with indecision. The lonely, wooded road slithered in front of her, cloaked by an ominous darkness. The forest had hollow spaces between the trees that just seemed to beckon something dangerous to hide there. Bears. Wildcats. Serial killers.

Molly shook her head. She was being ridiculous. She was an established, professional woman who should have long since outgrown her fear of the woods and nighttime. But some things never died. Memories from her childhood filled her, but she pushed them away. Not now.

Shakes overcame her anyway.

She looked in the rearview mirror and saw the red of her brake lights reflecting off the asphalt. Darkness swallowed everything else. Fear threatened to swallow her.

Whatever she'd hit still lay underneath her car. Her sedan had risen and fallen once, which meant that the front tires had gone over something, but not the back.

Probably just a deer, she rationalized. Perhaps someone else had hit the animal and left the poor creature in the road. The country lane was so narrow and winding, and outside was so dark. She'd rounded the corner and, just as she'd done so, seen a flash of something on the street. Before she could brake, she felt the thump against her wheels. The thump of a *deer* against her wheels.

Her throat went dry. She was going to have to get out of the car and check. Right?

Oh Lord, help me, please. I don't want to open this car door.

Why had she even agreed to come to the backwoods of Virginia's Northern Neck? What exactly had she been thinking when she begged for this temporary summer job in the middle of nowhere at Camp Hope Springs?

Closure, she remembered. She'd wanted closure, to go back to one of the happiest places of her youth. She had so many fond memories of her last summer of innocence, of being carefree and hopeful. Then she'd grown up and life had happened. Responsibilities had surrounded her and not let her go. She'd left her childhood behind right along with campfires and vesper services.

Her thoughts and reminiscing of the past only delayed the inevitable. She needed a plan, and she needed to get the yet-to-be-decided-on action over with. She rested her head against the steering wheel, flabbergasted by her own indecision. She couldn't simply sit here in the middle of the road all night.

The silver of her cell phone on the seat beside her caught her eye. She grabbed the device and flipped it open. What were the chances that she'd find reception out here? She blinked when she saw one bar left on her signal.

The cops. She could call the cops.

She lowered the phone to her lap. And tell the police

what? That she may have just hit a deer? They'd think she was crazy and rightfully so. She rubbed her forehead in irritation, staring at her headlights as they illuminated the deserted road before her. Camp Hope Springs was only a mile or two away at the most.

That settled it. She had to get out of the car and find out what had just happened. Just sitting here and thinking about the possibilities over and over would drive her crazy.

She grabbed the door handle and pulled until the latch clicked open. After taking another deep breath, she pushed the door out wide.

The smell of damp earth, of thick, wet leaves and tree branches ripe with moss and fungi filled the car. Crickets sang their songs. Leaves *tippity-tapped* together in the light breeze. Heavy summer air floated inside, covering Molly with its sticky, invisible fingers.

She fumbled through the glove compartment for a minute before finding a small flashlight. She twisted the top of it and a small ray of light sliced the air. It was better than nothing, she supposed.

She dropped one foot onto the ground and then the other. The woods still seemed to be staring at her, unknown dangers just waiting to pounce when she was least expecting it. She shivered despite the summer heat.

She squatted and shined her light under the car. Something off-white lay center beneath her vehicle.

A deer?

She moved her flashlight along the length of the creature.

Was that something blue? Maybe just the asphalt reflecting onto the deer's fur, she wanted to believe. And that splotch of white? Deer had white splotches, right?

She moved her flashlight up farther. Near her front bumper, her heart seemed to stop.

Eyes stared back at her. Not deer eyes.

Human eyes.

She'd hit someone. As a trained nurse she didn't have to touch the man to know that he was dead.

"I didn't see anything!" Molly insisted to the sheriff again. "I simply turned at the bend in the road and heard a thump. It was dark—frighteningly so." It was still frighteningly dark, she thought, wrapping her arms around herself. A chill seemed to emanate from the woods now and each whisper from the crickets seemed ominous, like those creatures knew something that she didn't.

They knew she shouldn't have driven through the woods at night.

The sheriff—a pudgy man with a soft jawline and full head of incredibly thick, dark hair—stared at her and then back at her car. Somewhere in the background, an owl hooted. The sound seemed almost mocking to Molly.

"The medical examiner is on her way. Maybe we'll have more answers then," Sheriff Spruill finally said. "Where did you say you were headed again?"

"Camp Hope Springs. I'll be working as a nurse there this summer."

"I'll need to talk to someone there to verify this."

"No problem. Gene Alan hired me. I'm sure he'll be happy to verify my reason for being out here at this hour."

"Gene Alan isn't at the camp anymore."

Molly blinked several times. "What do you mean? He hired me. Said I start tomorrow. When the campers arrive."

"No, he left about a week ago. Heard they got a new guy."

Great. Did she even have a job now? Where would she go if not to Camp Hope Springs? She'd given up the lease on her apartment. She had no job. No one else would hire her right now, not with the allegations that had been made against her—even if they'd been proven unfounded.

Headlights eased down the road, reminding Molly of two glowing eyes slithering toward them. The medical examiner? Molly wondered.

A pickup truck came to a stop in front of them. The vehicle looked much too old and beat-up to belong to the medical examiner. At least that's what Molly imagined. She watched as a tall man stepped out, his feet practically bouncing against the asphalt as he emerged. She blinked again as the man came into focus. She soaked in his messy, light-brown hair, the dimple on his chin, his worn, dusty jeans and the plaid shirt that was just fitted enough to show flat abs and broad shoulders.

"Nick White?" Molly nearly gasped as she said the word.

The man stepped toward her and squinted. "Molly Hamilton?"

"What are you doing here?" Molly asked, just as he blurted, "Why are you here?"

Molly stepped back, shock threatening to freeze her limbs and vocal cords. "You first."

"I work out here now. At Camp Hope Springs." He stared at her, unblinking, as if that same shock had overcome him. "Your turn."

The words seemed to stick in her throat. "I'm reporting for my first day of work."

"Out where?"

"At Camp Hope Springs." As soon as she said the words, she wanted to hide, to run. Surely Nick could see the vulnerability in her eyes at the mere mention of the camp. Certainly he knew how special the place was to her. He'd been part of the reason it was so special all those years ago.

Coming back here had been desperate and Nick would see right through her. Maybe she should turn and run and go back... Go back where? She had nowhere to go.

He rubbed his chin, his eyes looking perplexed. "Why in the world would you think that you needed to report to work at Camp Hope Springs?"

Why did he make it sound so outrageous? Maybe because he thought she wasn't religious enough to work at a Christian summer camp? "Because...because...they hired me to be their nurse for the summer."

His eyes narrowed. "I think I would know about that."

"Why's that?"

"Because I'm the camp director."

"Camp director? That's impossible. I would never have accepted the job if I'd thought you were the camp director!" Her hand flew over her mouth. Had she really just said those words aloud? She'd in no way intended to do that, but there was so snatching them back now.

"I guess I deserved that one."

The heat rose in Molly's cheeks. She hadn't intended on ever letting him know just how much he'd hurt her when he'd broken her heart all those years ago. But her old pain had risen to the surface. She'd just ended one relationship with a man who'd left her feeling belittled and weak. Being around someone else who'd broken her heart just firmed up her resolve for independence. She had to be strong, prove to herself that she was nothing like her mother when it came to men.

But a part of her wanted to turn around and run. But she wouldn't. She couldn't.

The two of them stared at each other.

The sheriff cleared his throat and they both turned to look at him. He shifted, as if uncomfortable. "Could we get back to the matters at hand now?"

Nick flicked his eyes away from Molly to look at the sheriff's car and then to Molly's sedan. His hands went to his hips just as his eyebrows drew together. "What matters would that be? What's going on here?"

The sheriff raised his chin and looked at Molly. "This young lady appears to have hit someone while driving out here."

Nick's eyebrows flicked up before his concerned gaze settled on Molly. "Hit someone?"

"I didn't hit someone. I mean, I did *hit* them, but I didn't *hit* them. They were in the road when I rounded the bend." She sighed, hating herself for getting flustered so easily. Nick had that affect on her. He always had. Why did he have to be here? Here she was, supposedly retreating from all of her problems, when a big problem showed up unexpectedly…perhaps the biggest one, bigger even than the investigation against her, bigger than the loss of her income and home, bigger than everything.

Nick had been her first love, the man who'd broken her heart and walked away from her ten years ago. And *that* was a problem.

Nick's eyes seemed to soften. "Is he…dead?"

Sheriff Spruill nodded. "Affirmative. The medical examiner is on her way."

Molly pinched the bridge of her nose. How had all of this happened? Just when she thought her life couldn't go downhill any more than it already had, it succeeded at sinking even lower.

What was that old saying? That the Lord had to make you hit rock bottom sometimes to get you to the place where there was nowhere else to look except up.

I'm paying attention, Lord.

"Any idea who he is?" Nick asked.

"No idea. Don't recognize him. Could be because he's under the car."

"He's still under the car?" Nick's voice rose in pitch.

"I didn't want to run over him more than I already did!" Molly felt her face heating. What was wrong with her? "Just in case…you know."

A respectable-looking white sedan pulled up behind Nick's truck. A middle-aged woman who walked with a slight limp approached them and introduced herself as the medical examiner.

After all the formalities were over, the medical examiner squatted down beside the car. "We're going to need a tow truck," she announced. "A tow truck with a very careful driver who knows how to get this car off the body without damaging it more."

The sheriff leaned down so he could peer under the car with her. "What can you tell from the body?"

"Based on the rigor mortis, I don't believe this woman killed the man. I think he's been dead for a couple of hours at least. I won't know anything for sure until I examine the body, however."

Relief flooded through Molly. Most likely, she hadn't killed the man. Most likely. Still, she wouldn't breathe easy until she knew for sure.

"Does that mean that Molly can leave?" Nick stepped up behind her. Molly felt his presence and her breathing quickened. She quickly took a step to the side.

The sheriff looked in the distance, as if in thought, before setting a steely gaze on Molly. "You'll be at the camp in case we have any questions for you?"

"Yes, sir." She glanced at Nick, quickly wondering if she had any other options. "I'll be at the camp if I am, indeed, hired, that is."

"I'll make sure she doesn't go anywhere." Nick glanced

at her again. His eyes weren't especially friendly, but they weren't uncompassionate, either. What were they? Still wide with surprise? A touch anxious?

The sheriff nodded slowly. "You'll need to stay in this area while the investigation is ongoing. Do you understand?"

Molly nodded. "Yes, sir."

"We'll tow your car in to get any evidence from it. We'll let you know when it's released. We'll also need for you to be available in case we have any more questions."

"Understood."

Nick nodded toward his truck. "Come on, I'll give you a ride."

Molly sighed. She was leaving one crime scene but entering another situation that seemed just as deadly…for her heart, at least.

An hour ago it had felt surreal to be driving down the rural Virginia road. By instinct Nick still expected to see the dusty, war-torn roads of Iraq as he traveled. He still felt on guard, waiting to encounter an improvised explosive device or to be surrounded in an ambush. That kind of conditioning took time to break, even as he was half a world away from the violence.

He'd only been back in the United States for a month, and he was still adjusting to this new chapter of his life. Though he was no longer a Navy chaplain, his military experiences would always be a part of him. He'd never forget the things he'd seen, the men and women whose lives had been changed. He'd been changed.

Up until an hour ago, that change had been his biggest thought. But now Molly sat next to him in his truck. They hadn't spoken since Nick broke up with her nearly a decade ago. He'd never expected to see her again, though he still thought about her often, wondering how she was, wondering if she'd ever understand why he'd had to break things off with her. Would Molly ever forgive him?

Nick didn't know the answer to that question, nor did he know if he even had the strength to address it now. When his last relationship ended six months ago, he'd realized that he was emotionally closed from giving his heart to someone else. He'd kept himself hidden behind taking care of other people for so long that he'd forgotten how to be vulnerable or to address his own needs. He wasn't sure he *could* be vulnerable. Taking care of other people seemed safer than trying to take care of himself. It was one of the reasons he'd come back here. Since losing his grandfather and his best friend within a year of each other, he'd shoved his own emotions into a dark corner. He had to address those issues and, until he did, his life would continue to feel stalled.

Did God bring Molly back into his life to remind him of his past failures?

Nick could see that Molly was nervous beside him as she twisted around in her seat. Her eyes looked red-rimmed, as if she fought tears. Her gaze fixated on something out the window.

He cranked the engine of his old clunker, left to him by his grandfather. "You ready?"

She shrugged. "I suppose."

They rumbled down the road in silence for several minutes. Nick had so many questions that each seemed to be on a collision course in his head. Why would Molly show up here? Why now? And why hadn't Gene mentioned to anyone at the camp that he'd hired someone as a nurse? Certainly the board of directors would have mentioned that to Nick.

Of course, if Gene hadn't left in such a hurry, maybe

the camp wouldn't be in such disarray right now. Maybe Nick wouldn't feel like he'd been sucked into the middle of a tornado, wondering exactly where he would land when the storm was over.

He had to say something to Molly. Even though the ride to the camp was only ten minutes, each moment of silence seemed to make the trip stretch on for hours. Long, painful hours.

He cleared his throat. "How are you, Molly?"

"I may have just killed a man."

"He was lying in the road, right? You wouldn't hold any blame for that. He was most likely already dead. That's even what the medical examiner said."

She shivered and pulled her arms more tightly around herself. "What if he wasn't?"

"Don't think like that."

"I mean, why would he just be lying on the road?"

"Maybe an animal got to him. Maybe he was trying to get to help when his body just couldn't take any more and he collapsed on the road."

"And I hit him…"

Silence stretched again. What did he say to that? Why *would* a man just be lying in the middle of the road? What explanation could there be for that? He tried to think of another, but couldn't.

"I didn't expect to see you here," Molly finally said.

"I didn't expect to see *you* here."

She didn't look at him, only straight ahead at the road before them as an uncomfortable tension stretched between them. "What happened to Gene?"

"He left unexpectedly." Gene was Nick's cousin and had always been a touch flighty. But leaving this way was unexpected, even for someone like Gene.

"I just talked to him last week."

Nick suppressed a sigh. "Last week is when he left." Nick had arrived back in the States a month ago, his military term completed. He'd retreated to the small home he owned forty minutes away from the camp. He knew he needed to rediscover his faith, which felt as tattered, worn and bruised as the battlefields he'd left in the Middle East. Instead, Gene had disappeared, and Nick had been thrust into the position of camp director. Upon his grandfather's death a year ago, this property had been left to Nick. Nick knew it was his duty to step up and run the camp instead of simply taking the advisory role he'd planned, but in doing so, he felt even more guarded than ever. He knew his heart had a big, gaping wound in it, one that needed time to heal. Instead, he'd been thrust back into the battle.

Molly shook her head. "Camp starts tomorrow. I can't believe Gene would cut out on you a week before the camp season kicks off."

"That's what everyone is saying. The board of directors is not very happy, to say the least. Gene never gave any indication that he wasn't happy here. It's like he just decided one day to up and leave. Left all of his things, even."

"Did anyone file a police report?"

"We let the police know what happened. The thing is, there's no sign of foul play. It just seems like he took off and left, following after another flight of fancy. Even Gene's family agrees. Sure, they're worried. But I guess we all expect him to come trotting back here any day now and tell us crazy stories about his latest adventures."

"Are you sure he left on his own volition?"

Nick swiveled his head toward her. "What are you suggesting?" His words weren't pointed, only inquisitive with a touch of surprise.

She shook her head. "Nothing. The accident is just doing weird things to my imagination, I suppose."

"The camp is a safe place, a place where kids go to find some peace, to meet God. It's not a place for fear or danger. It's a place of community, not..."

"Heartbreak. Judgment," Molly finished.

He could understand the jab about heartbreak, but judgment? Who had judged Molly? She'd always been well-loved, liked and respected. She'd risen above her circumstances, a hard childhood that included a neglectful mother who cared more about finding a new boyfriend than taking care of Molly. Still, despite those setbacks, Molly had become a strong, courageous woman who loved Jesus. What was there to judge?

Camp is a safe place, he repeated to himself. It suddenly didn't feel so safe anymore, not with Molly here to wreak havoc on his heart.

He approached the turn into the camp. His foot hit the brakes as the wooden sign proclaiming "Camp Hope Springs" came into view.

Pieces of the sign laid scattered in jagged pieces at the camp's entrance. Even from his perspective in the truck, it appeared someone had taken a chainsaw and ripped into it. Sharp, ragged chunks of wood were sliced and carved and slashed off.

Nick's heart sank. Could anything else go wrong?

He had a feeling he didn't want to know the answer to that question.

TWO

Molly straightened in her seat when she saw the destroyed sign. Her hands gripped the armrest beside her. "What happened?"

Nick threw the truck into Park. "The sign wasn't like this when I left for Bible study a few hours ago." He stepped from the truck and Molly scrambled out behind him. She decided she felt safer with Nick outside than she did by herself in the truck.

The sound of the woods enveloped them as soon as she set foot on the gravel drive leading to the camp. Aside from the battered sign, the entrance to the camp was just as she remembered it. A gravel road curved into the woods and she could barely see the lights that illuminated the camp's sidewalks twinkling through the trees. It was nothing fancy, nothing that would impress most people.

For a moment—and just a moment—it looked more enticing than a five-star resort. Then she remembered the events at hand all around her and the five-star resort image disappeared.

She stepped behind Nick and looked at the damage. The hand-carved wooden sign that once read "Camp Hope Springs" had been—violently, it appeared to Molly—

dismembered. Based purely on intuition, Molly knew whoever had done this had been angry.

She tried to find something comforting or sensible to say. Instead, she muttered, "Wow."

"Wow is right." Nick circled the mess, seemingly soaking in each detail. "I don't get it. Why would someone do this?"

"People do senseless things all the time. Maybe this is simply the work of vandals, or some bored teenagers who thought they didn't have anything better to do."

"I'll have to get this cleaned up before the campers come tomorrow." He ran a hand through his hair. "It will be one more thing to add to my list."

"I'm sure the rest of the staff will pitch in."

His gaze cut to hers. "Camp isn't like it was when we came here, Molly. Our numbers are down...way down. We've had to cut staff in order to make budget. I'm basically the staff here."

She twisted her head sideways. "Just you?"

"We have a part-time cook and a college kid who acts as lifeguard. A local man comes in once a week to cut the grass for us. That's it. The board of directors pitches in when they can. Local churches assign camp counselors and junior counselors as volunteers for their given weeks."

She shoved her chin up. "And me. You've got me."

A strange emotion flickered through his gaze. "And you."

"I won't stay if you don't want me to, Nick. I understand." Now why had she said that? She wanted to take back her words. Instead, she held her breath as she waited for his response.

He started back toward the truck. "No, you can stay. We need a nurse—a real nurse. You are a real nurse, aren't you?"

"I've been an RN for the past six years up at the naval hospital in Maryland. I'm plenty qualified." *And also just cleared of life-changing allegations of stealing drugs with the intent to distribute.* She kept that to herself. She knew she wasn't guilty and that she'd been cleared, but even the mention of the allegations could cause some people to question her innocence. At the least it could plant doubt in people's minds. Why bring up something that would only ultimately hurt her?

"You're hired then."

Despite the summer heat, Molly felt chilled from the feeling of unseen eyes watching her from the darkness around her. She always felt that way when the woods were nearby. Something about those trees, about the miles of nothing but forest, always had frightened her. She knew all too well how isolating that landscape could be, how one direction could blend into another until you didn't know where you were. She knew about the sounds of animals at night as they skulked around, looking for prey. The woods were no place to play around.

As they walked back to the truck, something popped in the distance. They both paused, and their gazes met.

"Was that gunfire?" Molly almost felt foolish for asking. Certainly that noise wasn't a gun. Not here. Not now.

Nick looked in the distance, his expression rigid and serious. "Sure sounded like it, didn't it?"

Another pop sounded, followed by a *ting.* Molly's gaze cut toward the noise and she gasped, raising a shaky finger at Nick's truck, right above the front tire. "Bullet hole."

Nick threw her to the ground, his body covering hers, just as another bullet sank into the side of his truck. "Has the whole world gone mad tonight?"

Molly's heart raced as she waited for whatever would

happen next. She turned her head toward Nick. "Why is someone firing at us?"

"I wish I knew. We've got to get out of here." He nodded at the truck. "Can you scoot under the truck to the other side?"

Molly nodded just as another gunshot sounded. Shivers raced through her as she pulled herself over the gravel and dust beneath her. The warmth of the truck sizzled across her back.

"You okay?" Nick remained beside her, placing himself between any bullets and her. At least the man was chivalrous, if nothing else.

Her throat felt as dry as the dusty road beneath her, but still she nodded. "For the moment."

"We're going to get out of this."

"What exactly is *this*?"

"I wish I knew."

She rolled from beneath the truck to the other side and waited for Nick to do the same. As he pulled himself out from underneath the vehicle, another pop cracked the air in the distance.

Nick pointed to his truck. "Get in. We've got to get out of here!"

Molly didn't argue. She dove into the truck through the driver's side and stayed low as she crawled over for Nick to climb behind the wheel. He sped off down the lane, throwing gravel as he did. It wasn't for another few minutes that Molly's heart slowed.

"What was that about?" Molly dared ask. "What's going on?"

Nick shook his head, the action looking heavy and weighted. "I have no idea. The sheriff is going to have a busy evening tonight, though."

"Was someone trying to kill us?" She trembled as the words left her mouth.

"I don't know about killing us. I do know that some-one's trying to send a message." He glanced at her. "We'll get this figured out."

Molly tried to shove those thoughts aside. All she wanted was to be somewhere safe. But could she feel safe here after everything that happened? With the man who'd broken her heart and abandoned her all those years ago? If her racing heart was any indication, then the answer was no.

Molly got another whiff of Nick's masculine scent just then. It was a mixture of mint and smoldering ashes from a campfire. The smell sent her back a decade. Nick hadn't really changed, not even his scent. Molly's gaze traveled to Nick's fingers where they gripped the steering wheel. They looked callused, as if he'd been working outside. He'd always been the perfect mix of outdoorsman and all-American boy—man now, she realized with clarity.

She cleared her throat, shoving down all of the emotions that had come rushing back to her. "All of this crime... isn't it unusual for this area? The camp seems so...peace-ful. At least my memories of the place are."

"It's very unusual. Nothing happens out here. It's just country folks who farm and work little local jobs. Quite honestly, I don't have time to deal with any of this right now."

Molly had a feeling that "any of this" included her. She decided not to say anything. Instead, she put her hands in her lap as the truck crunched over the gravel leading to the camp. Her eyes soaked in everything. It looked the same, even after ten years.

This wasn't a fancy camp where rich kids came as a luxury each summer. There were no tennis courts, horseback-riding lessons or rock-climbing walls. Camp Hope Springs was a little run-down, mostly with outdated buildings boasting cement floors, wood paneling and bathrooms that, even when cleaned, still appeared dirty. But for Molly, this camp was one of the first places she'd met God.

They passed the multipurpose building, named The Hill, where all of the classes and worship services were held. Beyond The Hill were the girls' cabins. On the opposite side of a huge open field were the boys' cabins. A pool surrounded by a chain-link fence waited beyond that. At the end of the drive, they reached a parking lot and the cafeteria.

"I forgot to get your suitcase. Not sure the sheriff would have let me take it anyway, until the scene is cleared," Nick said. "Maybe he can bring it when he comes to check out the gunfire."

Molly shrugged. "It's okay. I'll survive without it for awhile."

He nodded toward the cafeteria. "Come on. I'll show you where you're staying. I don't have time to be very sociable right now. There's too much to do before the campers show up tomorrow—including figuring out where those bullets came from. I apologize in advance for being a little preoccupied."

"Understood." She didn't expect him to be polite or sociable. She hardly expected him to be civil, but she'd take what she could get at this point.

She climbed out and followed Nick through a screen door. It slapped shut behind them, nearly making Molly jump out of her skin. Tonight had been one of those nights.

She stopped in her tracks as the room came into view. Wood paneling still graced the walls, lines of picnic-bench-style tables stretched across the room, the cement floor was painted red and a lopsided serving area occupied one corner. "Wow, nothing has changed, has it?"

Nick pulled his hands up to his hips and rested them there as he looked around the room. "Nope. We've been happy just to maintain the facilities. No money to upgrade them."

She touched one of the veneer tables, picturing herself sitting there at seventeen, eating bland spaghetti and canned fruit cocktail off plastic plates. "I never thought I'd be back here again."

"Too many bad memories?"

She averted her gaze to the floor. "Just the opposite, actually." She cleared her throat, realizing she'd said too much. "So where am I staying?"

"You're staying in the nurse's quarters. Right over here." He directed her to the back of the cafeteria, where a hallway led to the bi-level staff quarters, bathrooms, a lounge and, finally, the nurse's quarters. A small clinical area was at the front and a door separated that from the area where she'd sleep.

"I'll just make myself at home. I know you have other things to worry about right now."

He offered a clipped nod. "I appreciate it. I'll be upstairs in the office for the next few minutes, so if you need anything, let me know."

Molly nodded. Relief filled her when she was able to shut the door to her quarters and have a moment to herself. She had nothing to unpack at the moment. She simply wanted some time to compose herself.

She sighed and stepped toward the bathroom. Maybe a splash of water on her face would help refresh her.

Her foot hit the tiled floor. She stopped in her tracks and screamed.

The words "Get Out or Else" were written in red across the mirror.

Nick heard the scream from downstairs and forgot about the paperwork, the damaged sign out front, the flying bullets and even the shock of Molly's unexpected arrival. He took the stairs by twos in a rush to get to the first floor. Without bothering to knock, he threw open the door to the nurse's quarters. Through the doorway to the bathroom, he saw a pale-faced Molly staring at something out of his line of sight.

"What happened? What's wrong?" He rushed to her side.

She lifted a shaky finger and pointed at the mirror. Nick turned his gaze away from her and saw something written in red across the mirror. *Get out or else.*

He touched Molly's elbow, afraid she might pass out. "Let's get you something to drink while I call the sheriff."

"Why would someone write that?"

"We'll get to the bottom of it. Just hold tight." He led her to one of the cafeteria-style tables. "Let me get you some coffee. You okay with that?"

She nodded, her eyes still having a dazed look about them. He hesitated to leave her, feeling the need to be by her side. But he needed to call the sheriff. He hurried across the dusty cement floor into the kitchen, grabbing his cell phone as he did so. He prayed for service—which could be spotty out here—and dialed the sheriff's number. He lowered his voice when Sheriff Spruill answered and explained everything that had happened. As soon as the sheriff finished up at the incident on the highway, he said, he would stop by to file a report.

As he hung up, Nick grabbed a plastic coffee mug and poured a cup of stale coffee for Molly. He wished he could offer more, but this was the best he had.

He stepped into the cafeteria and immediately sucked in his breath again. He wished that Molly still didn't have that effect on him. But even after all of these years she still managed to take his breath away. Age had only made her more beautiful. Her auburn hair still shined and fell in waves around her face. Her porcelain skin appeared smooth and soft. Her blue eyes exuded kindness…and something else, too. Weariness? What had changed about her gaze?

He set the coffee on the table in front of Molly. She looked up, obviously startled. Her face still looked pale. Her hands still trembled so badly that he doubted she could even drink the liquid he'd brought her. He wanted to cover her hands with his own until the trembles stopped.

But Molly had given her heart to him once. He wouldn't be foolish enough to even pretend she could fall in love with him again, not after the way things had ended between them. Besides, Nick had settled on the fact that he'd never marry, that he had nothing to offer a wife. The walls around his heart were insurmountable. If someone did get past them, they'd be shocked and dismayed by the empty space on the other side. Deborah, the woman he'd dated for six months, had affirmed that. He was meant to give to others, but unsuited for the give-and-take of romance.

"The sheriff is on his way," he said.

"This is a nightmare. I should have never come. I don't know what I was thinking."

"Everything's going to be okay. The good thing about nightmares is that eventually you wake up. They don't go on forever."

The strain in her eyes as she looked up at him was

enough to make him back his chair away. That's what was different. There was something broken about Molly, he realized. Something that hadn't been there ten years ago.

"Yeah, that's what I've been telling myself," Molly murmured.

Now what did that mean? Just why had she taken a job here? And why had someone sneaked into the nurse's quarters to write that message on the mirror? It had to have happened between the time Nick left for Bible study and the time they arrived back at camp. Who could have done that?

Someone who was keeping a close eye on the place.

He resisted a shiver.

Nick had come here as a retreat, a time to reevaluate his life and his choices. He'd had no intentions of helping with the camp during that time because Gene was supposed to have a handle on those obligations. Nick knew he needed time to decompress after everything that had happened over the past year. First his grandfather had died. Then he'd ended his relationship with Deborah. A few months later, his best friend—another chaplain—had been killed by friendly fire while in Iraq. He needed to spend time seeking God before he figured out the next step in his life. So he'd stayed at his home and tried to block out life.

But now, it seemed like everything that could go wrong had. And it was only getting worse with each tick of the clock. First Gene had left unexpectedly, then an air conditioner went out, followed by the filter at the pool breaking, then two churches that had been big donors to the camp decided they couldn't financially support Camp Hope Springs anymore. And then there was today. Molly showing up and hitting a dead man, the sign at the entrance being destroyed, the flying bullets, and now this.

Suddenly, Molly stood, reminding Nick a bit of a cornered animal trying to escape captivity. "I want to leave."

"You can't leave. The sheriff ordered that you stay."

She shook her head. "You don't understand. I want to leave. I wanted a new start, not—not...not this. I just want peace."

"Peace doesn't come from the outside, Molly. It comes from the inside." Talking as if he was preaching a sermon seemed to come naturally. And he hated himself for it, even if what he said was true.

"You have no idea, Nick."

He sucked in a breath before rubbing his chin. "Actually, I do. Why don't you sit back down? Leaving now won't get you any peace. In fact, it would probably get you more heartache, especially when the sheriff finds out you violated his orders."

Her gaze skittered toward the door and then back at him. Finally, she nodded. "You're right. I just... I just..."

"It's okay, Molly. We'll get to the bottom of this."

She sat down and shook her head, some of the worry leaving her eyes. "You've still got it."

"Got what?"

"The ability to take chaos and make sense of it, to make people feel like everything will be all right. How do you do it?"

If only he could take his own advice...advice to let people in, to realize that getting hurt was worth the risk, that being misunderstood was a small price to pay for being authentic. Instead, he shrugged. "I just try to tell the truth."

She nodded again and looked away. Her fingers rubbed the coffee mug before stealing a glance at him. Her gaze looked tortured. "I'm sorry, Nick."

Sorry for what? For showing up here? For ever falling in love with him in the first place? Before he had a chance to ask, the front door opened and the sheriff walked in. Would Nick ever know the answer to that question?

No, he decided. He'd put as much distance between himself and Molly as humanly possible. He'd be busy with camp opening, so it shouldn't be a problem. His path would virtually never have to cross with Molly's. She'd be busy being a nurse, most likely hanging out in her quarters, while he'd be running around tending to everything else.

Guarding his heart should be perfectly easy and no problem. He'd perfected the act for the past ten years.

The sheriff nodded toward them in greeting. "The good news is that we just caught two hunters in the woods. They were both as a drunk as a skunk and without a license. We're fairly certain they're the ones behind those bullets earlier."

"Those shots didn't seem like that of a drunk man. They seemed purposeful, like they were aiming at us," Nick said.

The sheriff locked gazes with him. "Now why would someone do that?"

"I have no idea."

Sheriff Spruill turned his attention to Molly. "You sure you don't know that man who was hit?"

Molly nodded. "Positive. Why?"

"Your employment application was found in his pocket."

She shook her head. "That's ridiculous. I faxed that application to Gene a month ago." She paused, her eyes widening. "The man wasn't…Gene. Was it?"

"No, it wasn't. We'll have you take a look at the man in a few days to make sure you don't know him." The sheriff ran a hand over his face. He looked weary, tired and a bit overwhelmed. He should be. They hadn't had this much excitement in the county for a long time, if ever. "Now, where's this message that someone left you?"

"I'll take you," Nick volunteered. "You okay staying here by yourself for a minute, Molly?"

Molly nodded, her eyes still appearing hollow. He hesitated to leave her, but he wanted the chance to speak to the sheriff alone for a moment.

As soon as they were out of earshot, Nick leaned in close to the sheriff. "Any idea what's going on around here?"

"No, but I don't like it."

"Do you think that man was dead before Molly ran over him?"

"All the evidence indicates that he was. We still don't have an I.D. on him or an indication as to why he might have been lying in the middle of the road. The medical examiner said he most likely died from blunt force trauma to the head. Rigor mortis indicates that he'd been dead for twelve hours when that young lady had the misfortune of finding him."

"I drove down that road today. That man wasn't there twelve hours ago."

"Apparently the body was moved there."

They reached the nurse's quarters and Nick directed him inside to the bathroom. The message glared at him, sending icicles shooting through his veins.

The red color couldn't have been an afterthought. The message was supposed to look like blood, supposed to evoke fear.

The sheriff raised his eyebrows. "Now why would someone write that message here?"

Nick shrugged, hating to even think about that possibility. "Your guess is as a good as mine."

"You know the girl?"

Nick nodded tightly. "Yeah, we came to camp here together one year in high school." Nick made their friendship sound casual. However, at one time the two of them had talked about forever.

"Any reason why someone wouldn't want her here?"

He shook his head definitively. "Not that I know of. I haven't talked to her in years, though."

"More concerning than that is the 'or else' part of this message."

"Yeah, I don't want to know that means." An empty threat, Nick told himself.

The sheriff snapped a picture and then reached forward, touching a word slashed across the mirror. He pulled his hand back and examined his finger. He leaned forward and took a whiff of the liquid.

Nick waited to hear his analysis. "What is it? Paint?"

The sheriff shook his head. "No, I'm pretty sure this is blood."

THREE

"Blood? Real blood? Human blood?" Molly walked into the nurse's quarters just in time to hear the sheriff's proclamation. She felt the color drain from her face. As a nurse, she saw human blood all the time—but not human blood used as ink.

"Don't jump to any conclusions." Nick appeared at her side.

Jump to conclusions? What else was there to do but jump to conclusions? Someone was sending her a blatant, deadly threat. Since she'd just arrived, she had to wonder if the threat was directed to everyone at the camp and not just her, though. After all, Gene was apparently the only person who'd known she was coming, and Gene was nowhere to be found. What had she just walked into?

The sheriff cast his sagging eyes toward her. "Does anyone else know that you're here?"

Molly shook her head. "I told a few friends before I left that I was going away, but that was it. They didn't know that I was coming here."

"I'm assuming you didn't see anyone else at the crime scene? No other cars passed by?"

"No, no one." Just imaginary eyes watching her from the woods. But what if they hadn't been imaginary? What if those shivers she'd experienced had been because some-one really had been out there? She trembled at the thought.

Nick placed a hand on her forearm. "I think Molly's probably been through enough tonight. She needs to rest."

"We need to dust the place for prints, collect some sam-ples, take a few more photos. I'll send my crime scene guys out." The sheriff turned his gaze to Nick. "Anyone have it in for the camp?"

Nick flinched. "What do you mean?"

"The sign out front. This threat in the quarters. Maybe someone is trying to send a message."

"The camp doesn't have any enemies. None that I know of, at least. Of course I'm new here. I don't know exactly what happened before I came."

"You mean before the previous director disappeared?"

Disappeared? *Disappeared* seemed more ominous than saying the previous director simply left. Molly shivered again.

Nick visibly tensed and sucked in a breath, as if reality was finally hitting him. "Yes, that's correct."

"Who has keys to this building?"

"It wasn't locked. We usually don't lock up until 11:00 p.m. That's lights-out." Nick removed his hand from her arm and instead placed it on his hip, as if he was over the shock from the sheriff's questions and now ready to fight whatever was going on.

Sheriff Spruill nodded. "I'll put a call in to my guys now. You should have your room back in the next couple of hours."

Couple of hours? Great. What would Molly do for two hours? All she wanted was to be alone. Her dreams of curl-ing up in bed and trying to forget about, well, everything, obviously wouldn't be happening.

She'd stepped out of one nightmare and into another. Sometimes she just felt as if God had it in for her.

She shook her head. No, God didn't operate like that. God loved her, despite what happened in life. She constantly had to remind herself of that.

"Come on." Nick took a step toward the hallway door. "I'll find a place where you can be comfortable until your room is ready."

Good old Nick. He'd broken up with her all of those years ago because, basically, he was out of her league. He came from a picture-perfect family whose worst crime was skipping church while on vacation. Molly, on the other hand, came from a broken family who lived—to use the old cliché—on the wrong side of the tracks. Her father left when she was a toddler and her mother had turned to men and drugs to numb her problems. With no supervision, Molly had turned to partying to fill the gap. That was, until she'd gone to church with a friend and found Jesus. Her life had been turned around when she discovered what true hope was—*Who* true hope was, she should say.

When she and Nick had started dating, things had gone great for the first few months. They'd seen each other every weekend during the summer, going whitewater rafting with Nick's youth group, visiting the local amusement parks together and even working at a soup kitchen in downtown Richmond. Then Molly had started classes locally to become a nurse. Nick went to seminary three hours away. They continued to see each other on weekends whenever possible. But eventually, Nick had excuses as to why he couldn't make it back to town. The phone calls had become less frequent. Molly had known something had changed. She'd wanted, at first, to believe that he truly was busy with his studies. But then he'd called her, saying they needed to end things. They were two different people, he'd said. A long-term relationship between them would never work out.

Molly knew the truth, though. Why would she ever have thought that someone like Nick, from an affluent, well-known Christian family, would want anything to do with her? He needed someone as flawless as he was, and that person was not Molly. She refused to find her self-esteem in men, though. Her mother had been that way and Molly had seen the way it destroyed her life. Based on Molly's past relationships, making bad choices when it came to men must be in her blood. No, if she ever dated again, it would be someone who thought she'd hung the moon, who respected her and considered her an equal.

Not Nick White, in other words.

But despite their past, he'd always been kind. He'd always done the right thing. Always took a moment to pray before responding. Molly had thought he was the perfect man, a man who shared her heart for serving others in Christ. It was at that week of summer camp that she'd decided to become a nurse. After hearing a missionary speak, she decided she wanted to go and serve others in that way. Nick had felt the same calling to the mission field…or so Molly thought.

Molly wondered how he'd ended up back here. It wasn't that Christian summer camp wasn't a worthy place to be. She'd just never envisioned him working here as an adult. His family had pushed him to follow his dad's footsteps and become a pastor. She wondered about his journey from the time they'd last spoken. What had happened to lead him here?

"This way," he said, placing a hand on her back. Just his touch still sent a shiver through her. Why did he still have that effect on her? He led her toward the screen door. "Some fresh air sounds nice."

The last place Molly wanted to be was outside at night in the middle of nowhere. But at the same time, she didn't want to show her fear, for Nick to think of her as weak. So she sucked in a deep breath and prayed for courage as she stepped into the steamy nighttime.

"Feel up to a walk?"

Perhaps stretching her legs would be nice. Despite the thought, she still shivered as she said, "Sure."

She pulled her arms over her chest and soaked in her surroundings. Time hadn't touched this place. The camp even smelled the same, like old wood, fresh leaves and bug spray. "I feel like I've gone back in time. This place looks just like I remember it."

"It needs some upgrades, we just don't have the funding for them yet."

"I think it's charming."

"That's your nice way of saying run-down."

She smiled at his rakish grin. They kept steady pace beside each other, and Molly tried to assure herself that this stretch of wilderness was safe. It had been used for church groups and even local community clubs for decades. Still, prickles of fear danced across her skin and her throat felt dry as the lights of the cafeteria disappeared.

She cleared her throat, trying to distract herself from her growing fear. She needed to think of something safe—neutral—to talk about. "So, when are the campers coming to begin registration?"

A moment of exhaustion crossed Nick's features. "Tomorrow at three o'clock."

"What else do you have to do before they arrive?"

"The cabins still need to be cleaned, the snack bar stashed, the grass cut." He shook his head. "That's just for starters. The camp was practically in shambles when I arrived. I've been busy doing paperwork—preregistration for campers, background checks on counselors, making sure insurance information is up-to-date. I've been mending bunk beds, repairing broken toilets and patching roofs. I just haven't had enough hours in my day to get everything done that needed to be done."

"Things have a way of working out. I'm sure it will all get done."

"You've always had amazing faith, Molly."

His words reminded her that they had a past. But the conversation's positive spin conflicted with the way their relationship ended as, at the moment, he sounded like he admired her faith. In truth, he'd broken up with her because she wasn't good enough for him. No, he never said that out loud, but he didn't have to. His reasons were obvious. The thought of it caused turmoil to well inside. She needed to think about something else—anything else.

As silence fell, Molly's mind traveled to her time as a camper. "You know, everything that's happened tonight reminds me of one of those crazy campfire stories the counselors used to tell to scare us."

"Campfire stories were more fun when you were telling them as a counselor."

Campfire had always been one of Molly's favorite parts of camp, a time when it seemed like God and his creations met and hearts were touched as a result. But after the worship time was over and as people lingered around the fire waiting for the embers to fade, the scary stories emerged. Some of them still caused fear to taunt Molly. Despite that fear, talking about campfire seemed like a safer bet than other subjects. At least those scares were all of the make-believe variety. And at least they didn't involve her and Nick's past relationship.

"The one I still remember is the one about the prison inmate who'd escaped and still haunted these woods looking for prey." Molly shook her head. There was a federal prison only a few miles from the camp, so stories involving escapees were always a favorite. "I could hardly sleep at night thinking about those stories."

Nick smiled. "Chainsaw Charlie. A psychotic serial killer who escaped from the prison and lived in the woods around the camp. He always carried a chainsaw with him and liked to peek into the cabins at night, searching for his next victim."

Molly shivered just thinking about the story. "Then there were the supposed sightings of Charlie. I still remember one girl in my cabin started screaming in the middle of the night and said she saw Chainsaw Charlie peering in through her window."

"I remember that. All the cabins were on lockdown while the counselors checked things out. Turned out it was a boy who had a crush on her, if I remember correctly. He'd sneaked out hoping to get a moment with her and ended up getting sent home instead."

They passed the area of the camp that Molly called The Grove. It was an area of evergreen trees with benches along the outskirts. Molly remembered that this area was one of Nick's favorites, a place he'd often escaped to.

Campfire stories. She needed to keep talking about campfire stories and stop thinking about Nick.

"Then, of course, there was the story about Lucy Winslow, Chainsaw Charlie's victim." Molly shivered even thinking about the story.

"They say she still haunts the camp, upset she didn't finish out her week here. That, of course, we all know isn't true."

She glanced over at Nick's chiseled profile, one that seemed to beckon a second glance. "Was there a girl named Lucy who died here? I always heard that part was true."

Nick grimaced. "There was a camper here. She was fifteen or so. This was before you and I were ever here. Apparently, she was horsing around with some of her friends when she fell and hit her head. It was a freak accident. She did die, but it wasn't from Chainsaw Charlie. That's just how the story evolved over the years."

Molly shoved her hands into her pockets as they circled past the girls' cabins and began the walk back to the cafeteria. This was Camp Hope Springs, she reminded herself. Who would have thought in a million years that she'd be back here? And with Nick...

She cleared her throat, scolding herself for allowing her thoughts to go back to Nick. "Maybe counselors told us those stories so we wouldn't be tempted to sneak out at night."

Nick smiled. "It worked for me. Even with all of my logic, I had no desire to be anywhere near the woods at night unless I was with a group."

The path narrowed at the stretch ahead of them as the woods edged closer to the gravel. Molly pushed down her fear. "Seems like this could be one of their stories. Only this isn't a made-up story. It's really happening." She paused, ears straining to hear something in the distance. Was she hearing things? Had these stories caused a certain paranoia to rise in her?

"Molly? What's wrong?"

No, she definitely heard something...didn't she? "Do you hear that?"

"Hear what?"

"Listen."

Nick paused, quiet. A subtle noise sounded in the distance, causing both of them to freeze.

"Is that what I think it is?" he murmured.

Molly nodded, her face white again. "It's a chainsaw."

As the sound of the chainsaw intensified, Nick grabbed Molly's hand. His first instinct was to run toward the sound, to see who was behind such a cruel joke and put an end to this once and for all. But he couldn't ask Molly to go with him, nor could he leave her here on this path alone. Instead, he pulled her up the gravel pathway toward the cafeteria.

His heart raced, and he wasn't sure whether it was from the chainsaw or Molly's nearness. Most likely, it was both. "I need to get you back inside."

"Is someone just trying to scare us?" Her voice trembled slightly as the words poured out of her at a quick clip.

The woods blurred by them, but the chainsaw still growled in the background. "I'm not sure, but I'm not taking any chances, either."

Something was going on here at Camp Hope Springs, and Nick intended to figure out what it was. He'd walked into a mess, one that he hadn't created and hadn't chosen to get involved with. But despite those facts, he was here and someone had to deal with this chaos.

He urged Molly to walk faster, anxious to get her away from the person behind these threats. Whoever had that chainsaw was out in those woods right now. He was sending them another message on the evening before the camp season kicked off. Nick had never been one to give into bullies, and he certainly wasn't going to let this prankster get his way.

The chainsaw still squealed in the distance as they reached the cafeteria. Each nuance seemed to make his muscles tauter. Apparently, he'd left one danger zone in Iraq only to come here to another.

Just as he pulled open the screen door, a laugh bellowed out from the darkness. An evil, twisted laugh.

Nick's grip on Molly's hand tightened as he propelled her inside. "Come on."

The sheriff paused as he emerged from the staff quarters and stared at both of them. "Everything okay?"

Nick let go of Molly's hand, feeling foolish for even taking it in the first place. Grabbing her hand had just been pure instinct. "Someone's got a chainsaw outside."

"You saw them?"

"No, we can hear it. We didn't want to take any chances."

The sheriff looked back at two of his deputies. "Go check it out. But be careful. We have no idea what we're dealing with here. It could be a prankster but until we know for sure, we need to treat this as a threat of the highest level."

The two men headed out to their cruisers. Nick wanted to go with them. After all, this was the property his grandfather had left him. But as he looked at Molly's pale skin he knew he couldn't leave her, not after everything she'd been through tonight.

"Why would someone be using a chainsaw at this hour?" Molly asked.

Nick shrugged, trying to think of something— anything—that might calm her fears. He decided to go with the truth instead. "They want us to 'get out or else.' I'm just not sure why they want that, or how far they're willing to carry this."

Was there a connection between these threats and the man found dead in the road? Had he been murdered? If so, where did that leave Nick and the rest of the camp? Nick wasn't sure. He hoped these things were just a one-time affair, but what if they continued…?

The sheriff's gaze traveled back and forth between Nick and Molly another moment before he shifted his weight. "While my men are looking, I thought I'd let you know that your quarters are now clear. We've collected all the evidence we need. It will be a few days before we get any results."

Molly cleared her throat. "Thank you, sheriff."

A few minutes later, the two sheriff deputies emerged from outside. "There's nothing, sheriff. We don't even hear anything now. Whoever was out there is gone."

"I think we've done all we can do here. Hopefully, the evidence will turn up something. In the meantime, just be careful. Keep your eyes peeled and your ears open for anything suspicious."

"Will do."

"Call me if anything else happens. And lock up tonight."

After the sheriff disappeared, Nick turned to Molly and his smile dimmed. He started to place his hand on her arm, but stopped himself. They hadn't talked in years and things had ended badly between them. So why did it feel so natural to want to reach out and touch her?

He dropped his hand and shoved it in his pocket instead. "Why don't you get some rest, Molly? Everything else will get done in the morning. If worse comes to worst, we'll recruit some of the campers to help when they get here. And all that stuff that's happening? It's probably nothing, just some ill-timed and ill-advised pranks. But just to make you feel better, I'll lock up and check everything twice tonight."

Molly nodded, her eyes wide with uncertainty and a hint of exhaustion as she stepped away. "You know the area better than I do. I'll trust your opinion."

As she wandered back to her quarters, Nick had to

wonder if she should trust his opinion, though. Were these things just pranks? Certainly the dead body in the road wasn't. He hoped—and prayed—that there was some logical explanation for everything.

For the time being, he wanted to be by himself, to regroup. When he'd come back to Camp Hope Springs never had he imagined taking over the place. He'd wanted to find his footing and figure out his future.

He sat down at the cafeteria table, harder than he'd intended, and stared blankly at the screen door.

Since he'd arrived home, life hadn't been the retreat he'd hoped for. He needed to mourn the losses in his life. His most recent loss had been his best friend, Dewayne. He'd left one day to travel to a different location when friendly fire had gotten him. Why would God take away such a great man, a man who sought after him with all his being? Despite Nick's hurt, he'd had no one to go to with his pain. Deborah was right—he did have walls around his heart.

Those walls had started going up when he broke up with Molly all those years ago. He'd caved into pressure from his family. But he'd justified the decision by telling himself that he didn't want Molly to see who he really was. Because who he really was was someone who knew everything about acting like a perfect Christian when he hadn't touched his Bible in months or prayed other than to fulfill his studies. He acted like he had himself together on the outside, but on the inside he had a hard time distinguishing what was real and what wasn't.

This camp brought back so many memories. Molly's lovely face washed through his mind again and, against his better instincts, he smiled. She'd always been such a ray of sunshine in an otherwise dark sky. His mind went back a decade ago to that week at summer camp when they'd met. It had been more than her outward beauty that had attracted him to her. Molly had a way of forgetting about herself and her own problems and helping others. She'd been the first person all the other girls had gone to with their problems. They'd always known that their secrets would be safe with her. She just had a goodness about her, one that couldn't be faked.

He'd fallen in love immediately.

His heart still ached as he remembered the way it had all ended. As soon as he'd broken up with her, he'd regretted it. He'd told her they were two different people—and they were. Molly was too good for him. He frowned as he remembered seeing Molly for the first time on the road outside the camp, looking shell-shocked after running over the stranger sprawled across the asphalt.

He was so uncertain about so many things right now, but there was one thing he didn't waver about. Nick would make sure Molly was safe if it was the last thing he did.

FOUR

Molly sat on the lumpy, thin mattress she'd use for the next three months and braced herself for the beginning of a long summer that would certainly test her. It would be a summer of facing two of her biggest challenges—Nick White and the woods.

What a start to her time here. It couldn't be a coincidence that all of this was happening on the eve of the beginning of summer camping season. Someone had purposely planned to place these doubts in their minds on this evening. Molly didn't even feel confident that the hunters were the ones who'd aimed those bullets their way, despite the sheriff's conviction.

Even as the thought occurred to her, another slammed into her mind. The campers. Would they be safe here? What if someone revved up the chainsaws in the middle of the night while they were here? What if someone decided to take on the persona of Chainsaw Charlie and terrorize the campers? Even worse, what if a hunter's stray bullet wandered this way while the campers were here?

And why had her employment application been in that dead man's pocket? It made no sense. None of this made sense.

She tried to put the thoughts the rest, but couldn't. She

slipped from the nurse's quarters and wandered into the cafeteria. She paused in the doorway, spotting Nick at the table with his shoulders slumped. What had happened to him? What had changed him so much?

She cleared her throat, not wanting to scare him, especially after all that had happened. He looked over his shoulder and straightened. "Molly. Everything okay?"

She stepped closer. "I'm fine. I've just been thinking. Nick, do you think you should let the campers come tomorrow?"

"I've been wrestling with that thought myself."

"Do you think they'd be in danger by being here?"

"Right now we just appear to have some empty threats. I don't know if these are someone's idea of a prank or if there's more to it. Until we figure that out, I think camp should continue. I don't want to shut everything down just because someone's feeling mischievous or because some hunters had too much to drink and got trigger happy." His gaze stayed on her a moment. "What do you think?"

She paused, just a second. "I guess I agree. Until we have some answers, we should proceed. I just hope that things don't escalate."

"You and me both."

Awkward silence stretched between them. Why did you say to someone you hadn't spoken to in ten years?

"What a night, huh?" Nick finally said. He was apparently having as much trouble thinking about what to say as she was.

"You can say that again."

He opened his mouth and then shut it. Finally he ran his hand through his hair again. "Why here, Molly?"

She blinked, his question startling her. "Excuse me?"

"Why Camp Hope Springs after all of these years? I

never thought I'd see you again. I definitely didn't expect you to show up here."

Her throat burned at his words. "Camp Hope Springs is the last place I remember being happy. I wanted to have just a touch of that again. But I guess things aren't always the way we remember them being."

"I guess not." He stared at her, his face solemn. "You sure you're going to be okay? I know you're shaken up."

"I'll survive." But even as she said the words, there was a part of her that wondered about their truth. "How about you, Nick? Are you okay?"

"I don't know. I just know that I need a good night's rest. My ordered, predictable life keeps getting turned upside down. I'm beginning to not even trust my own instincts at this point."

Her heart ached at his words. "That doesn't sound like you."

"It's been a long time since you've seen me. Things have changed."

Molly looked away, deciding to ignore his comment. Though he had no reason to be angry with her, she had to acknowledge that skirting around the issue of their past could cause some heightened emotions. But Molly wasn't sure she was ready to talk about their breakup, to acknowledge those old hurts.

"I'm sorry." Nick raked his hand through his hair. "I don't know why I'm snapping at you."

"Don't apologize."

Molly wanted an excuse to not have to go back into the nurse's quarters. She knew she wouldn't be getting any sleep tonight as it was. There was no way she'd be able to relax enough to truly rest after all that had happened, especially when she thought about how someone had been in those very quarters. But she couldn't think of any other reason to be out here with Nick. She stepped back toward her quarters.

Just as she did so, Molly heard the screen door slam shut. She jerked her head toward the sound. A young man with shaggy hair and wild eyes stood there.

In his hands he held a chainsaw.

Nick stood as he saw Cody, the camp lifeguard, walk into the building. "Where did you get that chainsaw, Cody? And why do you look so crazy right now?"

"Sorry, the light just hurt my eyes for a second when I walked in." He raised the chainsaw. "I found this beside the pool when I went to check the pH levels there. I didn't want any of the campers getting hold of it tomorrow. You think Ernie accidentally left it there after he finished landscaping?" Cody set the chainsaw on one of the cafeteria tables and put a hand to his hip.

"I can't believe that Ernie would be that careless."

Could that be the chainsaw used to hack up the sign out front? The one he and Molly had heard from outside? He glanced at Molly and saw that her face was pale, listless. He realized that she had no idea who Cody was. It must have been a shock to see him there with what could be a weapon in his hands.

"Molly, this is the camp lifeguard, Cody. Cody, this is Molly. She's going to be the camp nurse for the summer."

At once, some of the tension seemed to leave Molly. Her shoulders eased down some, her lips cracked into a half smile. "Nice to meet you, Cody."

Cody nodded a greeting back to her. The nineteen-year-old had just finished his freshman year at college and fit the stereotypical lifeguard image—toned, tanned and blond. All of the female campers were sure to have a crush on him by the end of their stay here.

"You're going to need to leave that chainsaw with me. I'm going to have the police check it out." Nick explained about the sign out front, as well as the noises he and Molly had heard.

"That's odd. Why would someone destroy that sign? It's been there since I started camp here when I was a kid."

Nick nodded at the senselessness of it all. "My thoughts exactly."

"I hope the sheriff figures out whoever did this and gives him what he deserves. It's like the camp has been haunted or something for the past week—not that I believe in ghosts."

"What do you mean by that?" Nick asked.

Cody shrugged. "I don't know, man. It's just that the director cuts and runs, the sign is destroyed. I keep on thinking that someone's gone through my stuff in my room, even though there's been no one here. I just keep getting the feeling that someone is moving things, trying to send subtle signs that they've been there." He shook his head. "I don't know. That sounds crazy, doesn't it?"

"No. Thanks for sharing, Cody." Nick paused again. "You said all of this didn't start happening until Gene left?"

Cody shrugged again. "Yeah, man. Could be a coincidence. But maybe it's not. Who knows, right? I didn't want to mention it earlier because I didn't want to sound paranoid or something."

"No, I'm glad you mentioned it, Cody."

"For what it's worth, right? Anyway, nice to meet you, Molly." Cody glanced back at Nick. "I gotta get some shut-eye."

Nick drew in a deep breath. Why did he have the sinking feeling that Cody was anything but paranoid?

* * *

Molly checked the last bottle of medication and stored it securely behind a locked medicine chest in the nurse's quarters. That should be the last camper checking in. Middle school students had flooded the campus, ready for a fun-filled week at Camp Hope Springs. The bunch was already enthusiastic. Their excitement almost made Molly forget about everything that had happened the day before…almost. Fear still lingered in the back of her mind. What if what had happened wasn't an innocent prank? What if there was more to it? Were the campers in danger?

She sat back on an old couch in the room as shivers raced across her skin. She'd always had a good gut instinct for people and situations. Her gut right now told her that there was more to these "pranks" than just irresponsible fun. Could someone be so mad at the camp that they'd try to shut them down? Would these incidents remain pranks or escalate beyond that? Her presence here had nothing to do with this…did it?

Derek was the first person who flashed into her mind. Certainly he wouldn't have gone through all of this trouble just to make her life miserable and convince her to go back to Maryland.

Come back to me and I'll make the charges disappear, he'd said.

That's when she'd known that the false charges leveled against her were all a part of his plan to manipulate Molly into staying in a relationship with him.

Her anger over the situation had died and now she simply accepted it for what it was. She could do nothing to change Derek; she could only change the way she reacted. She'd learned through her troubled childhood that there were few things in life she could control, but her attitude was one of them. That very mindset—along with her faith—had gotten her through some of her darkest seasons.

A knock sounded at the door. "You ready for the staff meeting?"

She looked up at the sound of Nick's voice. "Is it that time already?" She stood and brushed the wrinkles out of her outfit, thankful that the sheriff had dropped her suitcases by this morning. "I've got all the medical forms filled out, so everything's good to go here."

Nick had scheduled a staff meeting to explain to all of this week's counselors that they should be extra vigilant and report anything suspicious going on. Would that be enough?

She joined Nick as they walked down the hallway to a meeting room. All of the volunteer counselors were waiting there, a good mix of youth pastors, college students and even a few parents whose kids were most likely horrified that they'd come along for the week.

Cody, the lifeguard, had recruited the young adults at his church to come to the camp right after service today in order to help clean things up. If it hadn't been for them, Molly wasn't sure things would have been ready for the campers. Cleaning the cabins was one thing. But the young adult group had helped to clean the cafeteria, the meeting hall and several of the picnic shelters in the area. Cody had taken care of the pool and cleared the campfire area and a few of the nature trails that had started to grow over. Ernie, the part-time groundskeeper who lived in town, had cut the grass. All of this after a makeshift church service in the meeting hall this morning.

So many memories of her time at the camp had flooded back to Molly. Her heart clenched as she remembered the good and the bad.

Her attention snapped back to the meeting. Nick stood

in front of the group, a picture of leadership and discernment. He'd always been a natural in front of people and his peers had seemed eager to follow. Things were no different now. Everyone's eyes focused on Nick, waiting for him to take the helm.

He hesitated a moment before stretching a smile across his face and welcoming everyone.

Molly watched him for a moment, knowing that she finally had the chance to soak in the changes the years had brought without seeming like she was staring. Time had been good to him and only enhanced his already handsome features. He had a few wrinkles at his eyes. He was still long, lean and fit. He had a few more chiseled muscles now than he did back in high school. His dirty-blond hair looked tousled. His blue eyes could still melt hearts, though their depths had taken on more layers.

What had really brought him back here? Molly felt certain there was more to his story. There was more of a hardness to him now. Had he simply grown up or had life taken a hard, unexpected turn somewhere down the line?

"I realize most of you were not expecting to see me here directing this meeting. The truth is, neither was I. Gene, the previous director, is no longer working at the camp, so here I am. I'm Nick White and this land was donated by my grandfather. I've served on the board of directors for the organization ever since I graduated from seminary, but I've primarily been deployed to Iraq with the Navy for the past six months," Nick announced.

Iraq. That was a place that could change a person. In her position as a nurse in a military hospital, Molly had specialized in helping veterans returning from war adjust to life back in the States. She'd seen how that place could change people, give them nightmares; yet, at the same time, purpose.

What had that time done to Nick, though? And would he ever let anyone help him?

The meeting concluded twenty minutes later. Ernie, the groundskeeper, leaned against the wall as everyone else cleared out of the room. Molly found her way over to him. The man was probably in his sixties, but still looked fit despite the deep wrinkles on his face, prominent because of his work out in the sun.

"I heard about what happened last night—all of it, not just the parts that Nick glossed over during the meeting," he started in a slow, country drawl. "You need to be careful."

Molly tensed. "How'd you hear?"

"One of the deputies was running his mouth down at the local bar once he got off duty." Ernie shook his head. "It's a small town. Unfortunately, people talk."

"Did they talk about who might be behind all of this?"

"You mean besides Chainsaw Charlie?" Ernie chuckled. "Did come up that none of this started happening until Nick White got back into town."

"I was with Nick when we heard the chainsaws. He obviously couldn't be in two places at once."

Ernie shrugged. "I'm just saying. I don't want to believe it, either. Maybe he's not the one behind these 'incidents,' but maybe they're happening because he's here."

"What sense would that make?"

"A lot of people would love this property. Who owns it? Nick White. Scare him off and maybe they have a chance."

"You really think someone from around here would do that?"

"I've lived around these parts for a long time. Sure, there are some locals who are up to no good and wouldn't think twice about going to great lengths to get what they want."

"I don't want to think people are capable of that." But she wasn't naive either, and she knew greed could cause people to do terrible things.

He nodded toward Cody, who stood off in the distance. "You might want to keep an eye on that young man over there."

"Cody?" she whispered. "Why would you say that?"

He shrugged again. "Had a reputation for doing drugs not too long ago before he started going to church. Drugs can make people do funny things."

"People change. Maybe he's put his old ways behind him."

Ernie held up his hands, as if in surrender. "I'm not trying to cause trouble. I was friends with Nick's grandpa, you know. I want what's best for the camp, too. What's best for the camp means clearing up this mess."

"Maybe it was all a coincidence."

"I don't believe in coincidences. Nope, especially not now."

The remainder of the day passed in a blur. Campers arrived, ate dinner, participated in a worship service and then ended the day with campfire. The songs soothed Molly's aching soul. The crackle of the fire, mixed with a single acoustic guitar and a multitude of middle school voices nearly brought tears to Molly's eyes. The simple worship, for a moment, made her forget about everything else going on—the reasons she left the hospital in Bethesda, the man she hit while traveling to camp, and being forced to work with the man who broke her heart.

What had Molly been thinking by coming here? Really, it had been a whim. She'd remembered Camp Hope Springs as a place of such peace and focus. She'd wanted that back in her life again, especially after what happened with Dr. Derek Houston... She shook her head, knowing she couldn't go there.

She wanted to put Derek out of her mind. Now that she was away from him physically, she had to remove herself mentally. He would not have an effect on her here, a hundreds miles away. But how did one get past the fact that you'd become everything you never wanted to be?

For so long, Molly had been strong and focused and had total trust in God. Then Derek came along and swept her off her feet with his charm. Slowly, that charm had faded and turned into subtle put-downs and control. She'd woken up one day with the realization that she was just like her mom—with a man who treated her poorly. Finally, she'd come to her senses and broken things off. Over the next couple of months, though, it had become apparent that she had to leave Maryland and Derek in order to regain her joy.

After campfire wrapped up, Molly gathered the campers who needed to take their medications to walk with them back to the nurse's quarters. Nick touched her arm, halting her, before she started down the path. She looked up, surprised at his closeness, drawn in by his expressive eyes framed by those long lashes.

"I'll walk up there with you. One second."

Relief spread through her. Fear still kept its sticky fingers around her, making the thought of walking anywhere alone seem frightening. Having Nick with them would help alleviate some of that anxiety—no matter how paranoid it might seem.

Nick chatted for a moment with a couple of counselors, giving them some instructions. As soon as he walked away, Molly missed his presence. Her emotions so easily fluctuated between hurt over their breakup to comfort in their easy companionship. Feelings were rarely simple, she'd concluded, and being with Nick only proved her theory true.

He jogged back over to her and, together, they led the group away toward the cafeteria. As they walked past the woods, Molly shivered again, a foregone reaction, one that she'd had since she was a child. She brushed aside the memories and plastered on a smile, unwilling to show the campers any fear.

Molly was the first of the group to step inside the cafeteria. The eerie quietness made her heart quicken a moment. The message left on her mirror yesterday flashed back into her mind. She swallowed the lump in her throat. Had someone come back this evening while they were at campfire?

No, no one had been in here since dinner, she told herself. The camp was safe and all the craziness of yesterday was behind them now. There was no reason to think otherwise. Quickly, the chatter from the campers filled the space, but Molly couldn't get the thought from her head.

Her hands trembled as she unlocked the door to the nurse's quarters. As the door opened, something flew into her face. Molly screamed. She scrambled backward, trying to disentangle herself from the object.

Nick jerked whatever it was off her. "What…?"

It was an old, ratty-looking doll with a missing eyeball and only patches of hair atop its head. "Chainsaw Charlie" was written in red across its body. Someone had hung the doll from the door, knowing it would fly in Molly's face.

"The pranks have already begun." Nick put a hand on her arm, his warm eyes assessing her. "I'll talk to the campers about it, let them know that pranks like these are unacceptable."

"You think this was a prank?"

He nodded. "This doll has been around for awhile. You

never know where it will turn up during any given week."
He ducked his eyes lower to meet hers. "Are you okay?"

"I'm just… I'm just surprised." She forced a laugh and
glanced at the wide-eyed campers beside her. "You guys
are going to keep me on my toes, aren't you?"

The campers let out a nervous laugh.

After everyone took their medicine, Nick and Molly
began walking the campers back to their cabins. She
gripped her flashlight as they walked down a particularly wooded, dark hill back to the girls' cabins. Her nerves
still felt on edge from the prank earlier. Would she ever
be able to relax here at the camp?

The kids didn't seem to be bothered by the isolation
out here, so why was Molly? She knew. She remembered
that time camping with her mom and her mom's new boyfriend. She remembered wandering off when her mom
wasn't paying attention. She remembered how easy it was
to lose your direction, for every tree and patch of under-
growth to look the same. She remembered the cold shivers that racked her body as night fell and she was alone…

Molly snapped from her thoughts and looked up. A
group had gathered outside of the girls' cabins. Tension
returned to her muscles. "What's going on?"

Tense lines formed on Nick's face. "Let me go find out."

Had someone been hurt? She pushed through the crowd
until she caught up with Nick. The dorm mom spoke
quickly, frantically. "All the girls are terrified," she explained. "Someone ransacked the cabins while we were
at campfire."

FIVE

Nick gathered all of the campers together on The Hill to have a long talk about pranks and to question each of them about who was behind the ransacking of the cabin. Most of the campers looked sleepy and confused. Even though Nick sounded stern, he also sounded relaxed, like he didn't want to scare anyone. Molly was pretty sure a few of the campers already wanted to go home, though.

Molly stood in the back, watching for a suspicious reaction, one that would hint of guilt. So far, nothing. Had one of the campers been behind the incidents today? Or was the same person responsible for yesterday's terror behind today's scares? Not knowing caused tension to embed itself in her muscles.

Laura, one of the counselors for the week and Cody's friend, paced to the back and stood with her. The counselor reminded Molly a bit of herself as a teenager. The two had already had some good conversations in their brief stay together.

At Laura's nearness, Molly's thoughts turned to Cody. Could he be behind these incidents like Ernie had suggested? He had the opportunity and means, Molly supposed, but what motive could he possibly have?

Laura leaned toward her. "Some kids never learn, do they? They only think about themselves."

Molly nodded. "At this age, believing middle schoolers can have maturity is right up there with believing in fairy tales. Hopefully, Nick's lecture will prevent any more of these incidents this week." *If a camper is behind any of this...*

"I was just a camper here myself last year. I never remember the pranks being this bad." She shivered. "They're actually starting to scare me. What if some psycho wants to get their kicks by bringing Chainsaw Charlie back to life?"

"Why would you think that?"

"It can't be a coincidence that the sign was destroyed with a chainsaw and that you heard chainsaws last night. It can't be." The college-aged girl shivered.

As the meeting wrapped up, Nick approached her. "Molly, will you walk all the girls back to their cabins and make sure they're all there and accounted for? I'm going to do the same for the boys. I'll walk back over and get you afterward so I can walk you up to the staff quarters. I don't want you walking alone, okay?"

Molly nodded, rationalizing that Nick was simply doing what was best for the camp. His concern over her safety had nothing to do with their past relationship or him still caring for her today. And even if it did, Molly knew they had no chance of a relationship together again, not after the way things had ended before. It was best to push the warm, fuzzy feelings that kept rearing up toward Nick into a deep place where they wouldn't emerge. She'd made the mistake of dating Derek. Now she had to reclaim her independence, to remember not to look for any type of security in a man.

She began ushering some of the girls toward the cabins.

Twenty minutes later, everyone was in their beds and accounted for. Molly stepped outside the cabin door, hoping that once she exited the building the campers would settle down. She'd wait by the door, under the sickly-yellow light where bugs swarmed, until Nick arrived. This way, she could see him coming and, if she stayed close enough to the cabin, she should be okay. No danger. No fear.

The crickets helped her to count the passing moments with their melancholy song. Mosquitoes and other nighttime insects buzzed. A few frogs groaned their midnight soliloquies. They were probably nestled along the swamp creek to the south of the camp. The mere thought of the murky water made her shiver.

What was taking Nick so long? She'd assumed he would be here by now, but he wasn't. As she swatted at another mosquito, she realized that maybe she should have waited inside.

"Molly." The wind rustled the tree limbs.

Chills ran up her spine. Had she just heard her name? It almost seemed like a whisper. Had Nick called to her? She squinted toward the distant darkness, looking for him, but saw nothing.

No, she must have been hearing things.

She pressed herself farther into the door, though. Her hand reached for the knob, ready to turn it and go inside if need be. Her heart beat steady and fast in her ears.

"Molly…"

She'd definitely heard her name that time. Her gaze darted around her, but she saw no one.

Where was the voice coming from? Not the cabins behind her, she felt sure. The voice called from farther away.

"Nurse Molly, help me. Please. I'm hurt."

She stepped toward the path, her throat going dry. Was someone hurt? It couldn't be any of the girls because Molly had seen for herself that they were all okay. Besides, the voice didn't sound feminine, more like a high-pitched male. Perhaps a prepubescent middle schooler? Were all the male campers accounted for?

"Please, Nurse Molly. I need you."

Sweat covered her brow as she stepped farther away from the cabins. Her urge to help someone clashed with her fear. "Where are you?"

"I'm over here. In the woods."

Molly paused, sweat trickling down her forehead. "What are you doing in the woods?"

"I was hiding, and I hurt myself. I won't play any more pranks. I'm so sorry."

The prickles deepened until they felt like spiders with needles for legs walking across her skin. She stared at the woods. "Why don't you come out so I can see you?"

"I hurt my ankle. I can't come out."

She stood at the edge of the trees now, but couldn't make herself go any farther. "I need to go get Nick to help."

"I'm not far away. Just a few steps. Please. It hurts so much." A little cry followed the statement.

Molly's heart lurched. Her gaze frantically darted around her. What should she do? She hated to think about a camper being hurt. But what if it wasn't a camper?

She touched a low-hanging branch as the damp scent of the forest rushed to her. "What's your name?"

Silence answered. Finally, a twig snapped. How close was the sound? Who had made it?

Shivers now claimed every muscle until even her teeth chattered. "Hello?"

"I'm here."

Her heart slowed a moment. "What's your name?"

The male's voice changed, sounding deeper, more gravelly. "My name is Chainsaw Charlie." A psychotic laugh bellowed, coming closer.

Molly darted toward the cafeteria. Adrenaline surged through her, causing each muscle to feel as springy as rubber. Was the man following her? She glanced back. Nothing. The next instant, she collided with something—or someone.

She screamed, visions of a masked man wielding a chainsaw claiming her thoughts. She had to get away before he pulled her into the woods, before he carried out his "or else" threat.

"Whoa. Where's the fire?"

Her gaze fluttered up. Nick. It was only Nick.

"What happened?" His gaze turned serious.

She sucked in a breath and pointed behind her. "Chainsaw Charlie."

Nick's gaze flickered behind her. "What are you talking about? Chainsaw Charlie isn't real."

"There…there was someone. He called to me. Said that was his name."

Nick's arms went around her. "Slow down, Molly. Tell me what happened."

She dragged in shallow breaths, trying to calm down. "Someone just called to me from the woods. At first he tried to make himself sound like a camper. When I got closer his voice changed. He said he was Chainsaw Charlie."

Nick's brows pulled together. "I'm going to get you back to the cafeteria, then I'll check it out."

"Could this be another camper prank?"

He shook his head. "All the guys are accounted for. Girls, too?"

Molly nodded. Nick's lips pulled in a tight line as he led her back to her quarters.

What was going on here? Molly mused with a frown. And with each "prank," Molly felt quite certain that these incidents were anything but.

After Nick made sure Molly was securely in the nurse's quarters with the doors locked, he ventured back outside. What was going on here? With each incident, his worry grew. What if these weren't pranks, but attempts to scare everyone away from the camp? But why would someone do that?

The sounds of nature enveloped him as he hurried back to the spot where he'd found Molly earlier. Chills raced across his skin. The damp scent of the woods—usually a comforting aroma—now put him on guard. Something was going on out there in the woods. He just had to figure out what.

He paced the treeline, not foolish enough to go into the wilderness alone at this hour. If he eliminated all of the campers and staff from these "incidents," that would only leave someone local. Plenty of people had reason to want them off of this property, he supposed. The camp sat on a four-hundred-acre plot of land and numerous people had tried to buy it up over the years, everyone from business owners to conservation groups.

He stood at the edge of the forest and listened. He heard an owl, a few birds and the ever-present crickets.

His muscles tightened. Was that a twig that snapped in the distance? Did an animal's weight break the thin wood? Or a human's?

His gaze zeroed in on something in the distance. A piece of paper was nailed to a tree. He trudged through the underbrush until he reached it. He plucked the paper down, squinting to read the words in the dark.

He sucked in a breath when the letters came into focus. *This is only the beginning.*

The rest of the week passed uneventfully, but Molly still wasn't able to put her mind at ease. Her only comfort was in knowing that all of the threats happening seemed to be centered on her and Nick and not the campers. She prayed that sheriff would catch the person behind everything and lock them away before any more harm was done.

Today was Saturday, her day off, as the first round of campers had left last night and the next round wouldn't arrive until tomorrow after church. She welcomed the break, though she had no idea what exactly to do with herself. She knew she had to pick up her car and hoped someone might give her a ride there. Otherwise, she planned to try and relax some.

After getting dressed, she wandered out into the cafeteria, ready to scour the fridge for leftovers for breakfast. She was surprised to see Nick there doing the same thing. Her first impulse was to retreat. They hadn't had many opportunities to interact during the week—only when needed. Maybe it was better that way. There was no need to bring up old hurts. Molly had let go of the disappointments of her past and she didn't expect closure or apologies.

Nick pulled his head back from the fridge, and Molly saw regret flash in his eyes. Sorrow about the past, or sorrow that he'd run into her today?

She put her shoulders back farther. "Morning, Nick."

"Morning. Hungry?"

"Starving."

"There's usually leftovers, but I can't find any this morning. I might have to cook."

Molly gasped in exaggeration. "Cook? What's that?"

He grinned. "What do you say? French toast and sausage?"

"You're going to cook for me also? I'm honored. Whatever you're making will be great, but I don't want to impose. I can grab some cereal."

"Don't be ridiculous. Cooking for two is just as easy as cooking for one."

"I won't argue." She leaned against the wall and crossed her arms as she watched Nick get busy.

"So, what did you think after your first week here?"

"I think I wish I had the enthusiasm and energy level I did when I was in middle school." She laughed. "But really, I thought it was great. You couldn't even tell that you've only been camp director for a week."

Something passed over his gaze. What exactly had happened before he came here? How had life changed him? There was now a heaviness about him, like he'd seen things that he carried around like burdens. He seemed subdued, like his thoughts were elsewhere.

She wanted to ask, but didn't have the relationship with him to do so. Instead, she went to the coffee pot and began a brew.

"The kids really liked you this week. You still have a way with people that amazes me."

She raised a brow. "What do you mean?"

He glanced back at her and shrugged. "You have a way of seeing through people to who they really are. People like the steadfastness in your eyes. They're drawn to your big heart."

Molly tried not to show her surprise. For a moment, it sounded like Nick actually thought highly of her. Could it be?

A moment of hurt crashed into her heart. He'd broken up with her, she assumed, because she didn't come from a squeaky-clean family. Her dad had left them. Her mom struggled with addictions. They were on welfare, and Molly was mostly left alone to fend for herself while her mother worked a dead-end job, spent time with another no-good boyfriend or recovered from a hangover.

No, Molly didn't have a flawless background. She'd always assumed Nick would ultimately want to be with someone who shared his background, who looked like the perfect Christian forward and backward, inside and out.

Nope, she wasn't perfect. But she did strive to follow God with all of heart, mind and soul. She'd come to learn that that was all that was required of her.

She turned away, afraid Nick might read her thoughts. She cleared her throat as she pulled down two coffee mugs. "We never did figure out who ransacked the cabins or who was hiding in the woods that night trying to scare me."

"Probably just one of the campers trying to get into trouble while away from home. I think every group that comes in here has at least one or two of those. Some kids are here because they want to be, and others are here because their parents made them."

"And some of those kids who are forced to be here actually leave changed. I guess that makes it worth it for all of the headache and trouble of the others."

"Agreed." He took a sip of coffee and looked at her over the rim of his mug. "So, what are your plans for the day?"

"I'm hoping I might pick up my car. The sheriff said I could get it back a few days ago, I just haven't had the chance."

He sat the coffee mug down and turned toward the sizzling griddle. "What's the update on the dead man?"

Molly shrugged. "They still don't know his identity. It's all very strange. This is a small county. The idea that a stranger is found dead in the middle of the road is un-settling."

"I agree." He flipped a piece of French toast. "I'll give you a ride into town. I have to do a few errands anyway. You may have to tag along for the first couple, if you don't mind."

Spending time with Nick brought both apprehension and curiosity. She wanted to know about his life since they'd last spoken. She wanted to find out if he was still the same person he was before. At the same time, she didn't want to get too close. "I'd love a ride. Thank you."

They sat down in the cafeteria to eat and chatted casually about campers, upcoming schedules and highlights from the past week. Casual. Impersonal. Safe. Molly could handle that.

Something about the moment caused her heart to un-expectedly, and abruptly, lurch. Though she'd long since forgiven Nick—at least, she thought she had—she knew part of the reason she'd never married was because no one had ever compared to Nick. She'd never experienced a connection like they had. But he'd proven that trusting a man with her heart would only lead to heartbreak. First Nick, then Derek. If a chaplain and a doctor weren't rela-tionship material, she held little hope that she'd ever find someone that was.

Her mom had once said, after one of her many break-ups, that men weren't trustworthy. None of them. Molly was beginning to think that was true.

She took another bite of her breakfast, trying to swal-low her thoughts.

She and Nick had no chance at a relationship again. The sooner she grasped that thought, the better.

Then why did the task feel impossible?

* * *

Nick saw the different emotions washing through Molly's eyes. What was the woman thinking? Would she ever forgive him for ending their relationship so badly? Would she ever understand why he'd done it?

He'd come back to the States ready to face his demons. He'd never expected his biggest regret to walk right back into his life again, though. God definitely had a sense of humor…or was it simply a great sense of timing?

He knew he needed to talk to Molly sometime, to explain himself, to tell her about the realizations he'd had over the last year. But now wasn't the time. He sensed something fragile about her now, a certain hurt in her eyes. What had happened to bring her back here? Certainly there was more to her story than she let on.

He wiped his mouth and stood. "Ready to roll?"

She nodded. "Thanks for breakfast. It was great."

Silently, they walked out to his dusty old truck. His grandfather had left it for him and it served its purpose here at the camp. It was really all that Nick needed since most of his time was spent right here on the campus.

He opened the door for Molly. As she climbed in, he caught a whiff of cucumbers and watermelon. He could bury himself in that scent, and, at the moment, wanted nothing more than to tuck her into his arms and let her presence consume him.

Of course, he could do none of that. They couldn't pick up where they'd left off. Even if Nick wanted to, Molly would most likely never forgive him and Nick couldn't blame her.

He wished he'd been strong enough to be his own man back then. Instead, he'd caved to the pressure around him. He'd given in to his hidden fears, fears that no one would have guessed…except maybe Molly. And that was precisely why he'd had to break up with her. She'd gotten beyond his walls, and that terrified him.

He pushed those thoughts aside as he climbed into the truck and cranked the engine. Cool air-conditioning blew through the vents at full blast, and again the scent of cucumbers and watermelons drifted to him.

That hadn't changed in all these years. Molly still smelled as sweet and innocent as ever.

As the truck bounced down the road, Nick decided to risk asking Molly about her past. The worst she could do was refuse to answer. "So, what's been happening in your life since camp, Molly?"

She shrugged and stopped examining her unpainted fingernails for a moment to glance at him. "What can I say? I went to nursing school, graduated, got a job. I worked at a Maryland hospital for six years and now I'm here. Pretty unremarkable, I'd guess."

"What happened to your dream of going overseas and being a medical missionary?"

Her lips seemed to pull down at the corners briefly. "Sometimes life gets in the way and you move on."

Questions swirled in Nick's mind. What had happened? How much should he pry? And how would things have turned out differently if they'd stayed together? Not only for Molly, but for Nick, too?

It didn't matter. As much as he'd like to believe his life could have turned out differently, he knew that he was his own worst enemy. He'd given so much of himself to other people that he had nothing to offer anyone else. He didn't foresee that changing any time soon. Sometimes, in fact, it felt like the walls around his heart were even higher and stronger than ever. Losing people you loved could do that to you.

Sadness pressed in on him at the thought.

Molly seemed equally as melancholy at the moment. Her eyes wandered the truck's cab until finally she plucked up a piece of paper that had gotten wedged between the seats. Nick's name was written crudely across the front.

"Looks like you've got some fan mail," she muttered.

He squinted. "I'm not sure where that came from." He pulled up to a stop sign, took the envelope from her and tore across the top of it. The typed words on the page made his heart stammer.

"What? What does it say?"

"It's from Gene. He said he's sorry for leaving so abruptly and please forgive him. He's decided that life is too short to work in a career that he doesn't love."

"At least we know he's okay. One mystery solved."

Nick looked over at Molly and shook his head. "Not quite."

"What do you mean?"

"Gene's last name is misspelled. Who misspells their own last name?"

SIX

"How is Gene's last name spelled?" Molly held her breath as she waited for his response.

"His last name is A-L-A-N. They spelled it A-L-L-E-N."

"What does this mean, Nick? Did someone hurt him and write this note to throw us off the trail? How long has this letter been there?"

He shook his head. "I haven't really driven anywhere in almost a week. Someone must have stuck the letter in here, but it got wedged between the seats."

She crossed her arms. "I don't like this."

Nick shook his head. "I don't like it, either. I'll drop this letter off at the sheriff's when we pick up your car."

Molly licked her lips, wondering what she and Nick would talk about now. Her thoughts whirled on Gene and everything else that had happened. Her first thought was that she should leave. But she knew she was too stubborn to be scared away. Even Derek hadn't scared her away from living up in Maryland. She'd left only after much prayer and feeling like leaving was the right thing to do.

"What are you thinking about?"

"I'm trying to think about anything but Gene right now."

Nick cleared his throat. "How's your mom?"

Molly's heart thudded with sadness. "She died two years ago." That's when she had met Derek. She'd been vulnerable and he'd stepped into her life at just the right time to swoop in and help take her worries away.

"I'm sorry, Molly."

"Me, too. But she battled cancer for four years. At least she's not suffering anymore."

"You were able to be there with her?"

"I was. She had no one else to take care of her. Her no-good boyfriend left after her first chemo treatment. He couldn't take it anymore."

"She never had good taste in men, did she?"

Molly let out a small laugh. "No, she always had awful taste. She seamlessly moved from one jerk to another." She'd always tried to find her self-esteem in men. Molly had told herself she'd never follow in her mother's footsteps. She'd watched the way men treated her mom, and vowed she'd never settle for someone who didn't respect her. In that sense, maybe it was good that Nick had broken up with her all those years ago. The past few years, however, had proven that she wasn't as strong as she'd thought.

"And *your* parents?" Even as she asked him, her throat felt dry. Nick's parents had never liked her. They'd had such high expectations for their son, and Molly didn't fit any of their standards. She didn't come from a good family. Her mom wasn't affluent, wasn't a churchgoer or respected in the community. On the other hand, Molly had found Nick's parents to be self-righteous, pious and too concerned with appearances.

"They're doing well. Dad's still the pastor up at Richmond Community."

"Church still growing?"

"Largest one in the city."

"I'm sure they're glad that you're back in this area."

He hesitated a moment. "They're not actually speaking to me right now."

"Oh," was all Molly could say. What had happened to fracture their relationship? Nick was their only son, and they'd had so many hopes for him. Molly had always wondered how Nick handled their overbearing nature so well. Whereas her mother had had no expectations for Molly, Nick's parents had had an overabundance.

They pulled to a stop in front of a hardware store. "I just need to pick up a few things."

"I'll tag along and stretch my legs, if you don't mind." Molly stepped out of the truck onto the dusty gravel parking lot. The summer sun beat down on them as their feet crunched against the rocky ground outside of the small-town store. Bells on the door handle jangled as they stepped inside.

Molly took a deep whiff of motor oil, spray paint and fertilizer. Something about the combination felt comforting and down-to-earth. Small-town America, she realized. She missed it. She'd been in Maryland for the past two years, living in an apartment only minutes from downtown. Being in the store made her feel like she'd returned home.

As Nick started down an aisle toward paint supplies, a round, robust man with a fringe of black hair called to him, stopping Nick in his tracks. "Nick White. When did you get back in town?"

Nick put on a good front, but Molly knew him well enough to know that he wasn't excited about conversing with the man who approached him.

"Wendell Manning." Nick extended his hand. "It's been awhile."

"You back at the camp?"

"I am."

"Never thought I'd see you back in this area. I thought you'd pulled up your roots and hightailed it out of here."

"I was gone for awhile, but I'm back now."

Wendell leaned toward Nick. "Funny that I ran into you because I've been wanting to talk to you. I'm hoping you might want to discuss the property that Camp Hope Springs is located on."

"What about it?"

"You interested in selling some of the acres? I'd like to expand the paper factory."

Nick shook his head. "My grandfather made it clear when he left the land for the camp that we couldn't ever sell any portion of it."

"I could give you a good deal. A deal good enough that you might be able to fix up some of the buildings on the property, maybe add a rock wall or a ropes course, update everything. Of all the acres the camp owns, how many are used? Ten maybe?"

"I can't change my grandfather's wishes, Wendell. You know how much he loved the forest—and how stubborn he was, for that matter. He made his intentions very clear. He wanted to preserve this land and there's no changing his will."

"There's always ways to get around legalities."

Nick bristled. "What are you suggesting, Mr. Manning?"

Wendell backed up, raising his hands in the air. "Not trying to offend you. I just thought it might be a win-win for both of us."

"Doing something illegal is never a win-win." Nick wrapped his fingers around Molly's arm. "Come on. Let's go."

Molly didn't argue, and Nick didn't say anything else

until they were inside his truck. By the way his veins popped out from his temples, he clearly wasn't happy.

"What was that about?"

"Wendell Manning thinks he owns this town. He's always thought that and will probably never change. Just because he's the richest man in the area doesn't mean he can buy his way around the law."

"I can't believe he even suggested that." Molly tried to phrase her next words carefully. "It's too bad that your grandfather said you couldn't sell any of the property. Some of that money would be really nice for the camp right now since it's struggling so much."

"I've thought of that before myself, but it just isn't an option."

"Why's the camp gone downhill, Nick?"

He shrugged. "I don't know what happened in the time that I was gone. Half of the members of the board of directors stepped down. Gene disappeared. Registration has been down. I guess Gene wasn't always the easiest guy to work with. Rumor has it that he ran off a few of the board members and ticked off a few of the churches that normally supported the camp, which is why registration is down."

"What did he do that was terrible?"

"He just wasn't a people person. I guess I should have been here and tried to referee things. Maybe I could have nipped this in the bud before it got out of control."

"You couldn't do that, Nick. You were stationed overseas."

He shrugged, the burdened look returning. "Yeah, I guess not."

A few minutes of silence passed. Farmland blurred past them, interspersed with patches of thick woodlands.

"What did you see over there, Nick?"

He jerked his head toward her. "What do you mean?"

"I see it in your eyes. Being in the Middle East changed you."

He shrugged, the action a little too forced to seem natural. "Being in a war zone does change you. Of course it does. But I wasn't even in the middle of the combat."

"Not physical combat, at least. I'm sure talking to all of those soldiers, helping them deal with their problems, was an entirely different kind of war zone. It was the war zone of the heart and mind."

"Yeah, but I had the easy job."

"I just have a feeling that you're holding things inside, like you're battling something on your own that's trying to defeat you."

"You talk like you know about it."

She shrugged this time. "As a nurse, I worked a lot with military returning from the Middle East. Of course they were hospitalized for physical injuries. But physical injuries seemed to just be a scratch on the surface. Seeing the things you do over there can make the most levelheaded person teeter on anxiety or post-traumatic stress."

"That's probably true, but I'm fine."

Molly was silent a moment before clearing her throat. "You always try to help other people and you forget about yourself. Sometimes you have to address your own hurts, Nick."

"You're assuming a lot, Molly."

"I don't think I am."

Nick didn't say anything else, and Molly wouldn't push him for answers. But more than anything she wished she could reach into his heart and treat it like she did a physical wound. Too bad it was never that easy.

* * *

Nick and Molly had just spent the last hour at the sheriff's department, explaining the note. The sheriff took the letter, said he'd check it for fingerprints and asked that they not share this information with anyone in the meantime. He'd also shown Molly a picture of the man in the road on the night she arrived. She didn't recognize him.

All along, Nick had hoped that everything that had been happening was some kind of misunderstanding or mischief. But he was coming to believe that there was more to it.

He drove solo back to the camp, Molly following behind him in her own car. As soon as Molly had gotten out of his truck and was safely tucked into her own car, Nick missed her. Which was crazy. Why did he miss the woman, who thought she understood him when she clearly didn't?

But she did.

If he was honest with himself, he would admit to the truth in her words. Molly still hadn't lost the ability to see through people's facades into their hearts.

And the last thing he wanted people to see was his wounded, battered heart. He'd put on a facade for so long, burying himself under the guise of carrying other people's burdens. Now was the time he was supposed to be tending to his own heart—being introspective about his upbringing, about the things he'd seen in the middle of war, about the detachment he felt from people, his inability to get close.

He hadn't realized his own issues until he dated someone who was just like him. He'd dated Deborah for six months. They were introduced by a friend who said they'd be perfect for each other. And in so many ways, they were. But one day Nick had woken up and realized that they were too much alike. They were both so guarded that they'd never really let each other in. He'd tried to talk to Deborah about his concerns, but she hadn't understood. They'd broken up and he'd gone to the Middle East. There, his best friend had been killed. Losing the people you loved hurt so badly... Was it even worth it? That's when he realized he needed to step back from his role as a pastor and counselor and figure himself out first.

Deborah, in the meantime, had found someone else to share her life with. Nick was happy for her. She deserved someone who could give her one hundred percent.

But would Nick ever be ready to give someone one hundred percent? Or would he always hide behind his mask as a counselor, a caregiver, someone that others leaned on? His time alone had only compounded his questions. Would he ever have an answer?

Even more reason to keep his distance from the straight-shooting, pure-hearted woman he'd at one time fallen in love with.

Had his heart ever really recovered from Molly? He'd tried to convince himself that it had, but the truth was that he didn't know. He hadn't ever loved someone like he'd loved Molly. The few women who'd caught his eye had never quite measured up to Molly's depth and compassion. She deserved someone who wasn't emotionally closed to others. That person wasn't him.

He pulled into the camp, a place that had so much potential. Would God really be able to use him here? Or was this just a temporary stop on this new journey he was on? He wasn't sure. He only knew he had to make the best of things here. He'd worry about his future later.

Nick walked into the cafeteria and spotted Cody standing in the kitchen. As he approached the lifeguard, Nick noted the puddle of water at his feet. Cody looked up and shook his head.

"This isn't good."

Nick braced himself for whatever news he was about to receive. "What's going on?"

"The refrigerator's out." Cody held up a bag of soggy lettuce and watched as water dripped from the corners. "All of the food is no good. All of it."

Nick stomped over to the commercial-grade refrigerator and peered inside. He'd just used that refrigerator this morning and it was fine. Worse yet, their food delivery had just come yesterday and the appliance had been fully stocked with a week's supply of food. Cody was correct, though. The inside wasn't even cool anymore. How long had Nick been gone? He glanced at the clock. Five hours at the most? "How did this happen?"

Cody shrugged and dropped the bag of lettuce into the trash. "I just got in. I came over here to grab some hummus I'd left and found this mess."

Nick checked the outlet. He reached behind the refrigerator and held up the power cord. "It's been unplugged."

The screen door slammed shut across the building. Molly stepped inside, pulling her sunglasses atop her head as she did so. She spotted them and paced over, her hands on her hips and her eyebrows knit together in concern. "Another so-called prank?"

A prank? Even Nick was beginning to see through that one. If this was someone's idea of a prank, then someone had a twisted—and expensive—sense of humor. "We've all been gone all day today. Someone must have come in and unplugged it after we left. There's no other explanation."

"I saw Wendell pulling in when I left this morning," Cody said.

Nick straightened and put his hands to his hips. "Wendell? When did you leave, Cody?"

"Not long after the two of you did. Maybe an hour later?"

"That would be about the time someone unplugged this fridge. Based on how quickly it lost its coolness, it's been off for at least a few hours." Nick shook his head. "We ran into Wendell earlier today. He must have stopped by right after we saw him at the hardware store. I wonder why."

Molly's gaze locked on his. "Maybe he wants to shut the camp down so he can buy the land. Maybe he's the one behind everything that's been happening here."

Nick shook his head and stared at the puddle of water again. "I can't see him being willing to sink that low. He's more the type who will try to find a legality that will have us kicked off the property than the type who will sink low enough to vandalize the place."

Molly shrugged. "I'm just saying, he's got the biggest stake right now in wanting this property. It would be smart to keep an eye on him. I think we've got to face the fact that someone is trying to shut this place down. The question is why."

Nick didn't miss the fact that Molly said "we." Knowing that she had his back in this whole situation brought him more comfort than it probably should. He pushed those thoughts aside to focus on the matters at hand. "The more urgent question is, how are we going to feed the campers this week? This refrigerator has been unplugged for at least five hours. We can't use anything in here and the camp just overdrew the account when the electric bill went through." Nick had some pay coming in from the military that he could use. But that pay wouldn't go very far to sustaining the camp, especially with all that had been happening here lately.

Molly nodded, a touch of determination in the action.

"I've got some money tucked away for a rainy day. We can use that to buy some more groceries."

"I can't ask you to give up your savings."

Molly shrugged. "God will provide. He always does. And he's providing for the camp right now. I believe in Camp Hope Springs. I'm not going to let someone shut it down."

"I appreciate your positive attitude, but I can't let you use that money. I should be paying you to be here. I can't let you pay for the camp's groceries."

"You're not going to let me. I'm simply going to do it, whether you like it or not." She raised her chin and locked her gaze with Nick's.

Nick had to suppress a smile because he knew there was no arguing with her once she set her mind to something. "You're one stubborn woman, Molly Hamilton."

"No, I simply know that God provides. He's proved that to me time and time again in my life. This instance is no exception."

Nick started to reply but drew his lips into a tight line instead. He wished he could have that kind of trust, but he didn't. Would he ever?

Three hours later, Molly, Nick and Cody had cleaned all of the spoiled food out of the refrigerator and made a new list of everything they needed to purchase before the next round of campers arrived tomorrow. With that list in hand, Molly climbed into Nick's truck with him, ready to head into town again and buy some food.

"Didn't we just do this?" Nick asked as they started down the road.

"At least this time Cody's at the camp to keep an eye on things while we're gone. It's a shame that someone has to stay behind to watch over the property like that."

"And Cody's only one person. The camp property is huge. But at least he can deter anyone from coming into the cafeteria and offices. Who knows what else someone has up their sleeve?"

Molly pushed herself back into the seat of the truck and let her thoughts roam free for a moment. "You really don't think Wendell would do this?"

Nick shook his head, his hands gripping the steering wheel. "I don't think he's the type. He may be shrewd, but I can't see him resorting to this."

"It wouldn't be very wise of him to do it after Cody spotted him coming to the camp. But why would he come to the camp right after he's run into you?"

"I plan on giving him a call to find out as soon as we get back."

"Is there anyone else who might want to see the camp shut down?"

Nick shrugged, the lines deepening on his forehead. "Not that I know of. Of course, I've only been back in town a few weeks. I have no idea what happened in the time I was in Iraq. Gene would know more than me. Prior to that, I was stationed down in Florida."

Molly shifted in her seat. "So what happened with Gene? I mean, what's the story before we found the note today? I heard the general version. How about a detailed one?"

Nick glanced over at Molly and shrugged again. "One Saturday he went into town for some supplies and he never came back. No one's heard from him since."

"He left all of his things here? I mean, if someone's going to take off on a new adventure in life, most likely they're still going to need their clothes."

"Yeah, he left everything. I left all of his stuff in his

quarters just the way he left it. The sheriff looked through everything, but came up with nothing."

"I thought it seemed suspicious before, but now I know it does. Something happened to him, Nick."

"My thoughts exactly. But until today there was no evidence that anything else happened to him. There's still no evidence of where he went—no paper trail, no phone calls, no travel brochures he left behind. None of this makes sense."

Molly had been tempted to leave without explanation when she'd come here. The drug allegations against her—though untrue—had tarnished her reputation and planted a seed of doubt in her coworkers' minds. The decision to come here had been impulsive. Most of her friends back in Bethesda had no idea where she'd gone. She'd simply told them she needed a change of pace. She didn't want to tell any of them her exact location in case Derek pressed them for information. Not telling them was the simplest option because she knew how persuasive Derek could be.

And Camp Hope Springs was certainly a change of pace.

Before Molly could say anything else on the subject, her cell phone beeped. She had a new text message. They must be getting close enough to civilization that she actually had reception again, unlike at the camp.

She flipped her phone open and saw the text message. Derek. Her heart sunk. She'd prayed that he would leave her alone. Hadn't he already caused enough damage in her life?

She braced herself for what he would say. As she read the words, her heart stammered in her chest. Come back to Maryland. Forgive me. Where R U? Can I come get you?

"What's wrong?"

She flipped her phone shut before Nick could see the

message. Her heart still raced from seeing the words. "Nothing. Nothing's wrong."

Nick raised his eyebrows. "Who was that message from?"

She shrugged, trying to appear nonchalant. She really didn't want to explain to Nick the headaches over the past year. "Just someone from back home. It's nothing."

"Well, judging from the way your face went white, it didn't look like nothing."

She squared her shoulders. "I don't want to talk about it."

Nick finally nodded, slowly. Molly had a feeling he wouldn't drop the subject, though. Maybe he wouldn't ask more questions now, but he'd ask more questions sometime. Should she tell him the truth? Would he understand? Once your reputation was ruined—even if by false rumors—a bad name seemed impossible to repair.

Thankfully, Nick didn't ask any more questions as they pulled up to the grocery store. Molly still needed more time to process Derek's message. Did he really think that Molly wanted anything to do with him after everything that had happened? Was he really that delusional?

Maybe Molly would simply keep her cell phone off for the remainder of the summer. That way she wouldn't have to worry about talking to anyone from her old job, especially not Dr. Derek Houston. She'd come here to get away from all of that.

Her hands trembled as she rested them on a shopping cart. She saw Nick take notice, but he said nothing. Good. If he wasn't going to share his problems with her, then she certainly wouldn't be pouring out all of her woes to him.

They decided to divide and conquer by splitting the list into two sections and each being responsible for half. That way they'd have enough time to pick up what they needed, pay and then head back to camp in time to sort everything and get ready for a new week.

Had Molly really been here for a whole week already? In some ways it felt like mere days and in other ways, like she'd been here all summer. Kind of like how in some ways she felt she'd been away from Nick for a lifetime, yet at the same time, it felt like it had only been weeks. Time had a funny way of playing tricks on you like that.

But a relationship with Nick would never be possible. Going back to him again would only prove she was just like her mom. No, she had self-respect. She wouldn't lose that again.

Not even for Nick White.

SEVEN

As soon as Molly disappeared on the other side of the store, Nick pulled out his cell phone. He couldn't get the look on Molly's face out of his mind. She was shaken. As if he needed further proof, the way her hands had trembled on her shopping cart was enough to make him want to pull the woman into a hug and offer to take all of her problems from her. But how could he even possibly help her if he had no idea what was going on?

He'd pulled out Molly's job application one night this week and noticed that she'd come here from a military hospital up in Maryland. He just so happened to have a friend he'd been stationed with over in Iraq who now worked there.

Forgive me, Molly.

As he dialed his friend's number, he glanced around once more to make sure Molly was nowhere nearby. She rounded the corner on the other side of the store, and Nick knew he had a few minutes of privacy.

"Mark Arnold, it's Nick White."

"Nick White! I heard you were back in the States and out of the military now. Who would have thought? The military lost one of its best when you left."

"What can I say? It was time for a change. It's good to be back home again. Listen, I have a favor to ask you."

"Anything. Shoot."

He glanced around again and lowered his voice. "I'm working with someone right now who used to work at your hospital. I need to see what you can find out about a nurse named Molly Hamilton."

"Molly Hamilton? That name sounds familiar. Is everything okay?"

"Everything's fine. I think there's more to her story than she's letting on. I was hoping you could find out something for me."

"You may not have saved me physically on the battlefield, but you saved me from myself on more than one occasion while we were deployed. I'll see what I can turn up."

"I appreciate it."

He hung up, satisfied that Molly was unaware of the phone call. Guilt began to nudge its way in, though. Maybe he should simply trust that Molly was here for the right reasons. When had Molly not been honest with him, after all? But his gut told him that there was more to the story and he intended to find out what. Something had her shaken, and he had a feeling it wasn't simply all of the vandalisms taking place at the camp.

Knowing he'd just lost some time, Nick quickly gathered everything he needed and then hurried to the registers to meet Molly. They both arrived at the same time with their carts loaded with food.

"I think this will hold the campers over for awhile." Molly smiled over the mounds of food in her shopping cart.

Nick couldn't help but smile also. "I think you're right."

"If someone thinks that unplugging a refrigerator, ransacking some cabins and hacking up a sign is going to shut down the camp, they have another thing coming."

Nick grinned. "They have no idea who they're dealing with, do they?"

"Not at all. Every new thing that happens just makes me feel more determined not to let whoever is doing this win."

"Are you sure you're not a good Samaritan that God sent here at just the right time?"

Molly grinned, but the smile quickly faded. "Quite certain." The troubled look returned to her eyes. Nick almost asked her what she was thinking, when a man appeared behind them in line. It was Richard Grayson, one of the camp's board members. The man's big hand clamped down on Nick's shoulder.

"Nick White, fancy seeing you here. Did you hear the news?"

Nick brought his hands to hips. "What news?"

Richard's loud voice boomed across the store. "They found Gene's car in the woods."

"Was Gene inside?" Nick braced himself for the answer.

"No, but there was evidence of foul play. Blood, for that matter. Lots and lots of blood."

Nick's eyes widened. *Blood? Was Gene okay? What had happened?* "Did the sheriff say anything else, Richard?"

The man shrugged. "It's an ongoing investigation. He can't share very much. I'm probably not even supposed to know as much as I do."

Now the man decided to be quiet and nonchalant. Nick wasn't finished with this conversation yet, even if they did have to have it in the middle of the grocery store. "Where did they find his car?"

"In the woods not far from the camp."

"Who found it?"

"Wendell Manning."

Nick sighed, deep in mucky thoughts. Wendell Manning's name had come up again. That couldn't be a coincidence. "I hope Gene's okay. I don't like this."

"He's a hunter. Maybe he went hunting. Maybe that blood isn't human blood after all."

Molly joined him, placing a gentle hand on Nick's arm. "We can only hope that it's animal blood."

Richard shrugged. "Maybe."

Nick tensed and not even Molly's sweet touch could sooth his frayed nerves. "What was your beef with Gene anyway, Richard? I heard the two of you didn't get along very well."

Richard looked around as if he didn't want anyone else to hear. His voice still sounded as loud as ever, though. "Gene was irresponsible. He didn't keep good records and I was always afraid he was going to get us in trouble with the IRS. He followed every whim—at least, he tried to. I felt like I was talking to a toddler every time we had a board meeting. And unfortunately, I had to take the role of parent and talk some sense into him before he drove the camp into a financial mess."

"The camp is in a financial mess. Are you saying it's Gene's fault?"

Richard leaned closer. "I'm saying he could have handled the money better. There are unaccounted-for sums of money missing from the camp's books. Gene is the person who had access to that money. It wouldn't surprise me if he took some of that money and ran."

"That's a big accusation, Richard. Why didn't you just go to the board with it? Or fire him?"

"Fire him? Then we get a lawsuit. We can't afford that."

"Why wasn't I informed of any of this?"

"You were in Iraq. We didn't want to bother you with it."

"I would think that's exactly the kind of thing that I'd be bothered with. My grandfather entrusted me with this camp after he died. I want to ensure that it's being run correctly, which is why we formed a board of overseers."

"We did the best we could, Nick. Half of the board members quit because they couldn't take working with Gene anymore. I was about to hand in my resignation when Gene left and you came back. Maybe he knew you were coming back and he saw this as a good opportunity to cut and run. I don't think that timing is a coincidence."

Nick had thought about that also. What if the timing wasn't a coincidence? All of this started happening after he returned. What would someone gain from Nick being back at the camp, though?

"I've got to check out before this ice cream melts. We've got a board meeting next week, right? We can talk about these issues then. This is only skimming the top of the camp's problems, though, Nick. I'm amazed you've been able to keep the place afloat since you've been back. I give you kudos for that."

"This camp was my grandfather's dream. He entrusted it to me." His grandfather had also been one of the few people who'd seen Nick for who he really was. His grandfather and Molly.

As Richard departed, Molly and Nick hurried through the line and paid for the groceries. When Nick saw the total, he nearly refused Molly's help. But he knew to refuse would be useless. Once Molly had something in her mind, there was no going back. But not even Molly's generosity could pull him out of his sour mood.

"Are you okay?" Molly asked quietly as they loaded up the shopping carts with bags.

"I don't know what to think anymore, to be honest."

"That was a lot to take in. This whole situation has been a lot to take in."

"You're telling me," he mumbled.

"Maybe you should hire someone to come in and do an audit of the camp's books and see what comes up. Maybe Gene was doing some shady things around the camp and that's why he disappeared."

"This just keeps getting worse and worse. I keep praying that all of these problems will disappear and instead they keep multiplying."

"What can I do to help, Nick?"

He shook his head. "Nothing. I'm sorry to dump this all on you. I'm sure you weren't expecting any of this, either."

"We'll get to the bottom of it, Nick. One way or another, we'll get to the bottom of it."

Yes, eventually the truth would come out. Nick just didn't want anyone to get hurt in the process. Especially not Molly. But how could he protect her when he didn't know what he was protecting her from?

They stepped back outside and into the sunlight. Nick squinted as they approached his truck, just as he heard Molly gasp.

He stopped in his tracks. His windshield had been smashed into a million pieces.

Someone was definitely trying to send a message, he realized. But just how far would they go to get their threats across?

Four days had passed with no new threats or incidents. But that didn't mean someone wasn't lurking nearby, about to spring on them like a lion finally claiming victory on its prey. In fact, the more time that went by without something else happening, the more unsettled Molly felt.

All of her fear culminated with Gene. What had happened to him? She felt convinced that he hadn't left of his own accord. Were the problems at the camp centered on Gene or the camp itself?

She hugged her arms across her chest and glanced across the darkening field, stealing a moment of solitude in what had been an otherwise hectic week full of high schoolers. The incidents from the week prior remained heavy on her mind. She couldn't stop thinking about who might be guilty or what had happened to Gene.

Could Cody have been behind all of this? Molly had a hard time believing it, but he did always seem to be nearby when something happened. He'd found the chainsaw, after all.

Board member Richard Grayson rubbed Molly the wrong way also. He'd seemed angry, and had made it clear that he didn't like Gene. Did he have hidden motives for wanting the camp closed? Molly wasn't sure, but she was happy that nothing else had happened.

She still shivered when she remembered that voice in the woods, though. She'd tried to set those thoughts aside and stay positive as the camp week had continued. Right now, the campers were broken up into their family groups, so Molly had taken the moment to slip away to one of her favorite places at the camp. Beyond The Hill was a field of wildflowers. Fireflies lit up the tall grasses as if a little piece of heaven had come down to earth. She remembered experiencing this magical sight when she'd come here as a camper. She'd been just as blown away then as she was now.

"Beautiful, isn't it?"

Nick's voice made her jump in surprise. Where had he come from? Her hand covered her racing heart. "I didn't hear you coming."

"Didn't mean to scare you. I'll try to whistle or something next time as I approach."

Molly smiled. "I guess I was just lost in the moment. I love how the fireflies form this little miniature universe here on the earth. It looks like the stars themselves have come down to earth for a visit. Creation is amazing."

Nick stood beside her, looking out over the field before them. "This was the first place I ever saw you, you know. Right here watching this very same thing."

Molly felt her cheeks heat. "Here?"

Nick grinned and nodded. "You were standing here on the first day of camp, looking at the fireflies just like you are now. You just looked so content. And unlike most of the girls at camp, you weren't afraid to be alone. You were confident enough to be by yourself and not intimidated by it."

"I think what you're saying is that I was a loner." She smiled.

"Not at all. You were just at peace with yourself. I saw that from the start in you."

She craned her neck toward him. "Why didn't you say anything to me that first night?"

"I didn't think I'd ever catch your eye. Not someone like you."

She turned toward him. "You could have dated any girl at the camp. I can't believe you would be intimidated by me."

"You were different."

Molly licked her lips as the memories flooded back. "Then we ended up in the same family group."

"And I couldn't pass up the opportunity since I figured it had pretty much been handed to me." Nick shrugged. "Besides, our first conversation centered around the proper way to eat watermelon—whether you should bite into a slice or use a fork and knife. I was hooked after that."

Molly tried not to smile. "You remember our first conversation?"

Their gazes met and Molly felt all of her resolve beginning to slip. Nick lowered his voice and reached for her arm. "Of course I do. I couldn't forget if I wanted to."

She turned away, her throat dry. "That was one of the best weeks of my life. Being here at Camp Hope Springs…" *With you.* She didn't say that last part. "It was incredible."

His hands slipped from her arm. "That was a great week. Then we launched off into the real world. It's a bit of a wake-up call."

Molly nodded. "Like cold water in the face, right?"

Nick chuckled. "That's putting it nicely."

So many questions floated through her mind. Finally, she grabbed hold of one. "Why aren't your parents speaking to you, Nick?"

The smile disappeared from his face. "They thought I got out of the military too early. And now my dad wants me to take a pastoral position at his church, but I'm not sure I want to do that."

"What do you want to do?"

He glanced down at the ground before looking back up at her. He shoved his hands deep into the pockets of his shorts. "I'm burnt out, Molly. I've seen things that still haunt me to this day. All I know is that I need a change. Working at my dad's church isn't going to cut it. If anything, it's just going to compound the way I'm feeling right now."

"It's good that you realized that. Not everyone would have. But I'm sorry it's caused a rift between you and your parents. I know they mean a lot to you."

Her heart rate quickened as Nick stepped closer. The look in his eyes took her breath away. "Molly, I just wanted to let you know—"

"Nurse Molly! Nurse Molly! Frankie just fell and hurt his ankle." Molly's head jerked toward one of the campers who ran down the path toward her. "He needs you."

She threw a quick glance at Nick, her throat burning as she did so. "I have to run."

But what had Nick been about to say? Would she ever know or had she just missed her once-in-a-lifetime chance?

It didn't matter at the moment. A camper needed her. Before Nick could say anything else, she took off in a jog.

The sun had sunk low now and darkness hinted its descent. A noise in the woods caused her breathing to quicken. She glanced beside her. A squirrel, she told herself. Just a squirrel scampering through the underbrush.

She continued up the trail when she heard something— or someone—stomping down the underbrush parallel to her.

She stopped. The sounds stopped also. Was she imagining things?

She took a couple more steps. A branch snapped. Underbrush swished. Breaking wood crackled.

Was someone following her?

She quickened her pace. She had to get to Frankie— now, if not for his sake then for hers.

With Frankie's ankle wrapped and iced and while the rest of the campers played a game of Faculty Hunt—a weekly tradition at the camp where the staff hid on the grounds, similar to hide-and-seek—Nick retreated to his office for a moment of quiet. Molly still affected him like no one else ever had. Thank goodness something had distracted them from the moment. He could never have a rela-

tionship with Molly again—that chapter had been opened
and closed. Even if she were to forgive Nick, he was des-
tined to be emotionally closed. He'd perfected guarding
his heart to the extent that he was at the point of no return.
He wouldn't hurt anyone else in the process.

The phone at his desk jangled and he picked it up, wondering if this call would be more bad news. "Camp Hope
Springs."

"Nick, it's Mark."

"What's up, Doc?"

"I did a little bit of asking around about Molly Hamilton. She worked here at the hospital up until about a
month ago."

"Okay." Nick had a feeling there was more.

"From everything I heard, she was a good nurse. Well
liked, a hard worker, personable."

That sounded like the Molly that Nick knew. His moment of relief was only short-lived, though.

"Unfortunately, there's more," Mark continued. "Someone made allegations that she stole some drugs. She was
cleared of the charges, but left shortly after the final ver-
dict."

Nick ran a hand through his hair. "Someone accused
her of stealing drugs?"

"The medications went missing on her watch. She
claimed her innocence all along and never once backed
down. Did you say she's working as a nurse for you now?"

"She is."

Mark paused a moment. "Does she have access to any
medications?"

"All of them." Nick's stomach sank at the thought.

"I'd keep an eye on her, Nick. There's rumor—and it's
just rumor, mind you—that she helped to take care of her
mother during her dying days and got hooked on some

prescription pain relief. That's what went missing at the hospital. She's the most obvious culprit, but the investigative committee couldn't find any hard evidence to prove her guilt."

Nick's heart sank. Molly a drug addict? He found that hard to believe. Not Molly.

But she had taken care of her mom during her last days. Molly had told him that much. And prescription drugs could be so addicting that even the most unsuspecting person could get drawn in by their lure.

He'd known that Molly was running from something, but he'd never dreamed that it might be this. He knew people could change, but being a drug addict didn't fit the image of Molly he had from years ago. Still, people weren't always the people you remembered them to be. Molly's mom had always had drug problems, but Molly had fought so hard not to be like her mom.

The last thing he needed at the camp was for someone to find out about Molly's past. If everything else that was happening here at the camp didn't shut the place down, an allegation like that could.

But he couldn't fire Molly. He rested his head in his hands a moment.

Oh, Lord, what am I supposed to do?

Before he could contemplate the answer, a breathless Molly ran into his office. Her eyes were wide and frazzled. "Nick, we have a problem."

"What's wrong?"

"We can hear chainsaws in the woods behind the girls' cabins. The girls are all terrified, Nick. They think Chainsaw Charlie has come to get them."

EIGHT

"We need to make sure all the campers are accounted for," Nick said, rushing toward the door.

Molly followed after him as he started down the hallway. On the way past Cody's room, Nick stopped. "Cody, go to the boys' cabins and make sure no one is missing. Tell everyone to stay inside. Then call the sheriff. Someone is using a chainsaw in the woods. This is just ridiculous."

Molly scrambled to keep up with him as he stormed toward the stairs. "You think this is a joke, Nick?"

He shook his head, visibly upset, judging by the tight line of his lips and his narrowed eyes. "I don't know what to think anymore."

Neither did Molly. How far could someone possibly take this? Now they were scaring the campers by bringing to life some of the old campfire stories that had circulated around the place for years.

They climbed into Nick's truck and took off toward the girls' cabins. As they got closer, the sound of chainsaws became louder. Nick and Molly looked at each other a moment. Finally Nick parked and opened the truck door. "Let's go check on the girls."

"I told them all to stay inside with the doors locked." Molly's hand gripped the door handle, but she froze, breathless at the thought of leaving the safe confines of the truck.

"Smart thinking." Nick glanced at her hand. "Do you want to wait in the truck?"

She couldn't wait in the truck, she realized. The parents of these campers had trusted her to take care of their children. This was no time to be a coward. "No, I'm coming with you." In one quick motion, she hurried from the truck to Nick's side.

Nick placed his hand on the small of her back as they hurried toward the cabins and rapped on one of the doors. "Open up. It's me. Nick."

The dorm mom answered, the woman's eyes full of fears, her hands trembling. "Nick, what's going on? Where are those noises coming from?"

"We're trying to figure that out. Are all of your girls accounted for?"

She nodded. "Everyone's here. Scared, but here."

"Listen, Amanda. I need you to stay calm. I want you to stay inside the cabin with the girls. Cody is calling the sheriff, and I'll be waiting out here until he shows up. Tell the girls that everything will be okay."

"They're frightened, Nick. I'm frightened." She ran a hand through her dirty-blond hair, leaving strands standing up on end.

Molly placed a hand on the woman's arm, forgetting her own fears as her instincts kicked in. "We're not going to let anything happen to you or the girls, Amanda. I'm sure this will all be cleared up soon. We just need to wait it out."

Nick's gaze fixated on Molly a moment, his eyes seeming to convey an unspoken confidence in her. "Stay here with them, Molly. I'm going to go check out the other cabin."

Molly nodded and forced a smile, trying to make

Amanda feel better. But the sound of the chainsaw in the distance tore at her nerves, each rev of the engine causing her heart to race and her blood to pump even harder. What was going on? And why was someone doing this? Molly had thought maybe the pranks were over, that whoever was doing this would leave them alone. No such luck. In fact, this was the worst incident yet.

"I don't know what to tell the girls—that they should run for their lives or stay put," Amanda said.

"Panicking is the worst thing they could do. The best thing right now would be a distraction. Sing some songs, play some games, pray—anything to get their minds off of what's going on."

Nick jogged back over, the moonlight casting its glow on his face. Normally, the picture would have been warming, but everything about this evening seemed eerie, like some unspoken sign that evil lurked nearby. "Everyone's in Cabin B also. I radioed Cody and he said all the boys are accounted for. He's called the sheriff. We're going to get to the bottom of what's going on."

A shriek cut through the air. Not the shriek of someone in trouble, but the shriek of a madman. Unwittingly, Molly grabbed Nick's arm, her heart jumping to her throat. "I don't like this, Nick."

Nick's face looked grim. "I don't like it, either." He turned to Amanda. "Get back inside. Lock the doors. I'm going to be out here, waiting until the sheriff comes. I'm not going to let anything happen to anyone, got it?"

Amanda nodded, her eyes still wide with fear.

Before she shut the door, Nick nudged Molly forward. "Go in there with them."

"I can't leave you out here alone."

"Of course you can. I don't want anything to happen to you—not that I really think this guy is dangerous. But just to be safe I want you inside with the doors locked and windows closed."

"But Nick—"

He leaned closer, close enough that Molly got a whiff of his woodsy scent. "Besides, I think you'll be good for the girls. You have a way of calming people down."

Finally, she nodded. If she could think of the girls in this situation instead of herself then she'd feel better. Taking the focus off herself always worked that way, even in the dire situation she'd been in at the hospital.

She squeezed Nick's hand before she slipped inside. *God, watch over him. Watch over all of us.*

Her throat felt dry as she clicked the locks in place, separating Nick from the rest of the group. He would be okay. He'd always been a good outdoorsman, and being in the military had to have given him great survival skills also.

She set aside those thoughts and glanced at the girls huddled up on the beds with wide eyes. Some had tears in their eyes as they clung to each other. The poor girls shouldn't feel this level of fear, especially at a place that was supposed to make them feel safe and closer to God.

She sat on one of the girls' beds and placed a hand on a camper's knee. "We're going to be okay. The sheriff's on his way and Nick is outside. Nothing's going to happen to us."

"Who's doing this?" one camper asked.

Molly shrugged. "I wish I could tell you, but I have no idea."

"It's Chainsaw Charlie. All those old campfire stories are true!" Another camper yelled. "He escaped from prison and now he wants to abduct one of us."

All the girls screamed and clung to each other again.

"Calm down!" Molly stood and waited until everyone quieted. "First of all, Chainsaw Charlie is not real. He's a character in a story that some counselor created just to scare campers. Second, whoever is making those noises in the woods is just someone who wants to scare us. We can't let them win. We need to stay strong, okay? Like they talked about at chapel tonight where God says we shouldn't worry. How about we pray together?"

A few girls nodded uncertainly. Molly held out her hands. "Come on, everyone. Let's get in a circle. Everything's going to be just fine."

Molly squeezed the girls' hands beside her in the circle and closed her eyes, praying to God that He would calm their fears and bring the person doing this to justice. Molly knew she was praying for herself just as much as she was praying for the girls.

God, help us feel your mercies...

Nick was amazed at the difference in the girls when Amanda opened the door to Cabin A. Gone was the feeling of panic from earlier, and he even heard a couple chirps of laughter. He had a feeling Molly had a lot to do with the change. The woman was a force to be reckoned with.

His heart quickened when Molly came into view. It didn't matter that things had ended poorly between them. It didn't even matter that she had drug theft allegations against her. He couldn't deny that the woman still had a way of making his heart race, of taking his breath away and of making him want to be a better man.

She shoved her hands down into the pockets of her jeans as she approached him. "What's going on?"

He cast aside his thoughts and focused on the matters at hand. "The sheriff has his men out there combing the woods, but I'm not sure how much they'll find. I haven't heard the chainsaws in at least thirty minutes so my guess is that whoever was doing this is long gone." He looked beyond her to the empty bunk beds. He guessed all of the girls were huddled together in the center of the room. Thank goodness they weren't screaming and crying anymore. "How are the girls doing?"

She glanced behind her and lowered her voice. "They're okay. We prayed about it and now they're playing a game."

His smile disappeared as footsteps sounded behind him. He took a step back when he saw Sheriff Spruill approaching, a grim look on his face. "Can I talk to the two of you in private?"

Nick offered a curt nod. "Of course."

The threesome walked several feet away to a picnic shelter. The sheriff's eyes looked serious, like he had bad news, as he glanced up at them. Tension embedded itself deeper into Nick's muscles as he braced himself for whatever the sheriff might share. "What's going on?"

The sheriff swallowed before slowly moving his gaze between Nick and Molly. "My men haven't found anything in the woods yet. Everything that's been happening at the camp makes it seem like someone wants to scare you away from here. Nick, I have to ask, is there anyone who would benefit from getting you off this land?"

Nick and Molly looked at each other a moment, and Nick knew they'd both had the same thought. Wendell Manning. He was the most obvious person who wanted the camp's land. Nick cleared his throat before telling the sheriff about their conversation in the hardware store a few days earlier, as well as the subsequent power outage in the kitchen where all of their food had spoiled.

The sheriff jotted the information into a notebook before looking up again. "Anyone else?"

Nick shrugged. The thoughts had been circling in his mind for the past couple of weeks, so he didn't have to think too hard about his answers. "As you know from the

incident a couple of weeks ago, we've had some problems with hunters on the property. They get too close to
the campsite and we've been nervous that a stray bullet is
going to come from the woods and hurt someone."

"We'll question them again, see if we can get anything
else out of them."

Nick drew in a breath. "Then there's Richard Grayson,
who's a board member here. He said that he had some concerns about Gene mismanaging some of the camp's funds."

"Is there any evidence that that's true?"

Nick shrugged. "I know the camp is on the verge of
shutting down. I haven't had a chance to decipher all of
Gene's less-than-stellar record-keeping yet, though."

"If you have a chance to do that, let me know." The
sheriff's gaze turned to Molly. "How about you, Ms. Hamilton? Any enemies?"

"M-me?" She stammered, her eyes widening with surprise. "Why would it make a difference if I had any enemies or not?"

"Because none of this started happening until you arrived here." The sheriff locked his gaze on Molly.

Molly's face drained of all its color and her former calm
seemed to disappear quicker than the morning fog. "I...
uh...I don't know."

Sheriff Spruill raised a brow. "You don't know if you
have any enemies?"

She licked her lips and heaved in a deep breath—
probably a quick prayer, too, if Nick had to guess. Some
of her calm returned. "There is one person, I suppose, who
might be considered an enemy." Her gaze flittered to Nick,
but only momentarily. "Derek Houston."

"Tell me about this Derek Houston."

Her face remained expressionless. "He was someone I
knew up in Maryland."

"A boyfriend?"

She nodded, but the motion seemed weighted down and hesitant. The questions had her flustered, which piqued Nick's curiosity. Who was this Derek Houston? And why did the man have this effect on Molly? Nick felt a wave of both protectiveness and jealousy as he waited for her responses.

"Yes, he was my boyfriend. We broke up a couple of months ago."

"And why might he have something against you?"

She rubbed her hands on her jeans before drawing in another breath. "He was the Chief of Staff at the hospital where I worked as a nurse, and he's used to getting what he wants. I made him angry when I broke up with him. He was very persistent, to say the least."

"I see. When was the last time you spoke with Derek?"

"He texted me this past weekend. I didn't respond, however, and I don't believe that Derek knows where I am. I don't see him as the type who'd be in the woods with a chainsaw, however. He'd have other ways of trying to make my life miserable."

What did she mean by that? Anger flashed through Nick at the thought of someone trying to make Molly's life harder, but that anger was immediately replaced by guilt. Nick had broken her heart. That ranked high on the list of offenses toward someone.

Despite Nick's guilt, he still felt of a rush of protectiveness toward Molly. Did this doctor have anything to do with the prescription drugs that Molly was accused of stealing? Nick could ask her, but that would only make Molly think that Nick didn't trust her. It would show her that Nick had checked up on her past.

"If you hear from him again, will you let me know?" the sheriff asked.

Molly nodded. "Of course."

"Do you think we should shut down the camp, Sheriff?" Nick asked. He held his breath as he waited for the sheriff's response. Nick had to ask the question. He didn't want his stubbornness to put someone's life in danger.

Sheriff Spruill sighed, as if deep in thought. "No, not yet. I don't believe anyone's in danger. I think someone's just trying to scare you. But if this keeps going on, you might want to consider it."

Nick nodded, praying he was doing the right thing by keeping the camp open.

Please, Lord, keep everyone safe. Watch over them. And drive away this darkness that's trying to close in.

Molly tossed and turned in bed that evening as imaginary chainsaws crept into her hearing. When she wasn't hearing things, she was mentally replaying her conversation with the sheriff. Why did he have to ask about her enemies? She hadn't wanted to bring up Derek, and she especially hadn't wanted Nick to know about the man. Derek was a part of her past that she wanted to leave behind— permanently. But Derek had always been persistent. What had made her think that quitting her job and coming here would change anything?

As soon as the sun peeked over the horizon, Molly threw her legs out of bed, ready to get started for the day. Anything beat being alone with her questions, rehashing her regrets and wanting redos of the past. Though she tried to extinguish her worries through prayer and Bible reading, the flames only seemed to be doused temporarily.

After grabbing some coffee, she headed to the flagpole in the early sunlight hours. At 8:00 a.m. every day, campers gathered there to say the Pledge of Allegiance and morning prayer. Molly liked to arrive early for some quiet time of her own. Once the day got started she barely had a moment to breathe as campers were around her, asking questions, wanting a listening ear, desiring attention. She was more than happy to give them those things, as long as she was able to fill herself up in the morning with some time alone first.

She sat down on the already sun-warmed bench and pulled her legs underneath her. Crickets chirped in the background and the sun's rays reminded her of lemonade pouring over the ground. A line of ants had begun their march across the concrete, breadcrumbs in tow. For a moment, everything seemed right. Life continued forward, just like the little insects hurrying past her feet.

This morning was so different from last night. This morning, everything appeared peaceful and back to normal. The camp, even with everything shady that had been going on lately, reminded her of a little slice of heaven on earth.

She read her Bible a moment and said some morning prayers. As she said "amen," her gaze traveled upward to the blue sky above. The feeling of contentment that had settled over her quickly fled as her gaze fixed on something.

At the top of the flagpole, a noose flapped in the breeze. She squinted. Inside the noose hung a doll with red hair that looked strangely like Molly.

She sucked in a gasp when she saw the white nurse's uniform the doll wore.

That doll was supposed to be *her*.

Who would do such a horrible thing?

NINE

At the sight of the first campers walking down the distant pathway, Molly quickly yanked the doll down. After everything that happened the previous night, the last thing the campers needed was to be frightened further by seeing that atrocity.

Molly's gaze skittered around her, looking for a place to stow the doll, but came up empty. As the campers neared, she shoved the doll and rope between herself and her Bible. She hugged everything to her chest, hoping no one would notice. As the campers called their sleepy hellos, Molly forced a smile.

Nick's broad form lumbered toward the flagpole. He wore his customary plaid shirt and jeans, looking handsome in the outfit. His hair, still wet from the shower, already had its customary spikes. Just seeing him brought Molly a certain measure of comfort. Nick. He'd make things better. He always did.

As soon as Nick arrived at the pole, he glanced her way. His eyes soaked in her stance before traveling back to meet her gaze. Molly saw the question in his eyes. She tried to silently tell him that she'd explain later. Molly had never been in such a hurry to get through their ritual around the flagpole, though.

Lord, forgive me, she prayed silently, *for wanting the campers to rush through prayer.* But the noose seemed to burn through her clothes, to sear her skin.

As soon as the campers were dismissed for breakfast, Nick stepped closer. The scent of fresh soap and piney shampoo filled her senses as he stood close enough to touch. "What's going on, Molly? Why are you hugging a doll and a rope?"

She looked around, making sure all the campers were truly gone, before releasing her hold on the objects. They tumbled onto the bench beside her. The sight of them made her throat go dry once more. "I found this hanging on the flagpole this morning."

Nick stared down at the objects with eyebrows drawn together in a scowl. "A doll with a noose around her neck?"

Molly nodded, her heart pounding in her ears as blood rushed through her veins. "A doll that just happens to have auburn hair and green eyes, just like me. Not to mention the outfit."

Nick's gaze pierced hers with so much intensity that Molly stepped backward. Whatever he was feeling, it was strong and fierce. "Molly, maybe Camp Hope Springs isn't the best place for you to be."

She flung her finger into her chest. "You think this is my fault?"

"Not at all. I'm worried about you, though, especially after seeing this doll. Someone's trying to send a message. I'd like to believe it's just an empty threat, but what if it's not?"

Molly dropped her hand and raised her chin. "I'm not going to let someone scare me off, Nick. They're not going to win that easily."

Nick's eyes softened. "I don't want to see you in dan-

ger, Molly. We don't know who we're dealing with here.
Maybe it's no one. But what if there's more to it?"

Molly had thought those same questions. She'd felt the
fear try to overtake her. But she wouldn't let it. "Nick, I
don't like what's going on here either, but I'm not going
to let that change anything. I'm staying put." She crossed
her arms over her chest.

He stared at her, something unsaid in his gaze. Finally,
he took a step back. "I can't make you go. But I want you
to be careful."

A car rumbled down the road at that moment, and both
Nick and Molly turned toward the sound. As far as Molly
knew, they weren't expecting anyone today. The sedan
braked in front of the two of them and a moment later an
older couple stepped out. Molly had seen them before, but
couldn't immediately place them.

Nick dropped his hands from his sides. "Mom? Dad?
What are you doing here?"

Nick's mom stepped toward him, uncertain emotions
passing through her gaze. "Nicholas, why didn't you tell
us about the note Gene supposedly left?"

Nick's dad stepped up behind his mother, a tall, broad
man who still carried himself like a soldier. "We thought
you would let us know about something like that."

Nick raised himself up to full height. "The sheriff asked
me to keep it quiet. How did you know?"

"The sheriff told your aunt Emma Jean that you'd found
it." Accusation tinged his mother's voice, causing Nick's
skin to bristle.

"I didn't know it was public information yet, Mom. I'm
just trying to do the right thing."

Silence fell heavy and thick. Finally, his mom turned

her gaze from Nick and glanced beside him. "Molly Hamilton?"

Molly showed what appeared to be a forced smile. "That's me. Hi, Mrs. White."

"I never thought we'd see you again." They *hoped* they'd never see her again, Nick thought wearily. "What are you doing here?"

Molly kept her chin up, not one to back down—just one more quality that Nick admired about her. "I'm working as a nurse here for the summer."

Nick's mom looked back and forth between the two of them before finally putting her hands on her hips and narrowing her eyes. "She's why you came back, isn't she? You gave up what could have been a distinguished career in the military for her, just like we warned you not to do."

Nick mirrored his mom and put his hands on his hips. "I didn't even know that Molly would be here, Mom. And besides, Molly would have been worth coming back for. Don't talk about her like she's not here."

His mother looked away, anger sparking from her eyes. Nick's dad handed her a tissue and she carefully dabbed under her eyes. Finally, she appeared to compose herself enough to turn her glare back to Nick. "She's always been a bad influence on you, Nicholas. She's rebellious, mouthy and she'll bring you down. I only want what's best for you."

"Honey." Nick's dad put his hand on her shoulder, trying unsuccessfully to restrain her from whatever words were about to pour from her lips.

"No, I need to say this." She jerked away from her husband, fire in her eyes. "Why would you give up everything for this place? Why won't you accept the position at your father's church?"

Nick kept his shoulders square, not wanting to hurt his

mother, but unwilling to let her walk over him anymore. "Mom, I don't know what I want to do yet. I need some time to figure it out. It's not personal. Please don't take it that way."

Her arms dropped from their sides and her chin rose. "I see. Is that how you're justifying all of this? We've sacrificed everything for you, and this is the thanks we get? We paid to send you to the best schools and colleges. We've supported you and organized drives to collect stuffed animals for the children in the orphanages in Iraq who had captured your heart. We've only provided the best for you, and now you embarrass us like this?" She turned on her heel. "Come on, Fred. Let's go. I can see we're not wanted."

"Honey—" Mr. White started.

Nick's mom slammed the car door instead of responding. Nick's dad looked up with apologetic eyes and offered a slight wave as he climbed in after his wife.

And as quickly as they'd appeared, they left.

What a disaster. And poor Molly. To have to hear his mother talk to her like that.

"I'm sorry, Molly," Nick started.

Molly shoved her hands into her pockets and nodded slowly, thoughtfully. "That was ugly."

"I know."

"Seeing me here didn't do anything to help."

He stepped toward her. "I don't want you to read anything into what my mom said, Molly."

"I've always known she didn't like me, Nick. That was no secret."

"My mom…" He shook his head. "She just wants to build this perfect little world around herself where she's in control of everything. As their only son, I guess I played a pretty big role in that world. I've only got one chance at this life, though, and I can't let someone else make decisions for me. I have to answer to myself and, even greater, answer to God."

"You're right. You can't let other people call all of the shots." She tilted her head at him. "Your mom seems pretty intent about you working at your dad's church."

"They felt confident that I would take it, and even let the news leak to the congregation that I'd be working there."

"Have you had any more thoughts on the job offer?"

"I'm not in a good place to minister to others, Molly. I can't even be honest about my own flaws. I can hardly admit my own weaknesses or struggles. It's too easy for me to put on masks when I work in ministry. I want to be…authentic."

Molly smiled. "I'd say you just were."

"He's still working on me."

"How did you come to realize all of that?"

He looked in the distance, toward the woods. He shrugged. "Primarily through a relationship with someone just like me."

Before she could respond, another car pulled up. The sheriff emerged from his sedan. Maybe he had some news for them. And maybe it was better to simply end this conversation now.

Nick raised his chin in greeting. "Sheriff Spruill. What brings you out here?"

The sheriff approached Molly, his weary eyes pulling down at the corners. "We have a name for the man you…collided with…on your way to Camp Hope Springs. I thought you'd want to know."

Molly's entire body seemed to tense as she nodded. "Definitely. Who was he?"

The sheriff looked down at the pad of paper in his hands. "His name was Hans Huber, and he was from

Germany. So far, no one knows what he was doing here in town. We're trying to contact his family now to get more details."

"He was from Germany?" Nick tried to let the information sink in, while sorting out whether or not that fact had any significance.

"He's lived there all of his life. For some reason, he was in the States and he had your application. We'll figure out why eventually."

Molly nodded again. "Thanks for letting me know. I know his family must be wondering where he is."

Sheriff Spruill turned his gaze to Nick. "We weren't able to figure out who was behind the chainsaws last night. We found some footprints and took molds of them. I can say that Wendell's whereabouts were accounted for last night, so we know it wasn't him. He and five of his friends were playing cards until the wee hours."

"Thanks for the update, Sheriff," Nick said. He reached over and took the doll from the bench. "We found this on the flagpole this morning."

The sheriff examined the doll for a moment before shaking his head. "Someone's definitely trying to send you a message."

Nick placed his hand on Molly's back, wanting her to know that he was here to support her. "We've gotten the message loud and clear."

The sheriff raised an eyebrow. "You're not going to take heed of the warning, I take it?"

Molly shook her head. "I'm staying right here."

Finally, the sheriff nodded and took a step back toward his sedan. "So be it then. Do be careful. I don't want these incidents to escalate."

"Neither do we," Nick assured him.

Molly wrapped her arms over her chest and looked into the distance as the sheriff pulled away.

More than anything Nick wanted to protect Molly—both her heart and her physical well-being. But he wasn't sure which would be harder.

Molly shoved her hands down into her jeans pockets as she turned to face Nick. Her thoughts swirled around in her head with an almost dizzying effect. Even more than the sheriff's warning, Nick's mom was knocking her off balance.

The woman always had a way of making Molly feel small and insignificant. She hadn't failed to deliver again today, and given Molly the harsh reminder that she wasn't good enough for Nick—never had been and never would be. Molly just hadn't thought it would hurt so much now that she was an adult. She'd thought she was past that, but apparently not because all of those old emotions threatened to rise to the surface again.

And then there was Nick's revelation about working in ministry. She wanted more than anything to get to the bottom of what was going on with Nick. What had happened in his life? What had led him back to Camp Hope Springs? And what were his plans for the future? Was he walking away from ministry or was he walking away from God? And why did hearing that Nick had been in another relationship cause a touch of jealousy to sweep through her?

"You okay?" Nick looked down at her with that soft, compassionate look in his eyes that used to melt her heart.

She nodded while swatting away a fly. "I'm just processing everything." She pulled a loose hair behind her ear and shrugged, uncertain of what to say. She finally settled with another shrug and, "You know."

"Even if you don't want to run because of the craziness

going on around here, I wouldn't blame you if you did. After all, who expects to walk into something like this? You came here to do a job that you were hired to do and, on top of that job, you have to deal with everything else that's been going on. Most people would have left after the first week."

"Well, I'm not most people." She tried to smile light-heartedly, but the look in Nick's eyes made her lose her breath a moment. His eyes seemed to draw her in, to mesmerize her. Before she blurted something she regretted—something like "I could still fall in love with you"—she changed the subject. Because, despite whatever warm, fuzzy feelings she experienced at the moment, she would not allow herself to run into any man's arms again. She had to prove she could stand on her own two feet.

"How about you? You think I've been thrown into the middle of this? You've been not only been thrown in, but the whole mess has drawn you in with very few escape options."

A slight smile cracked his otherwise serious features. "This was my granddad's dream. I can't let it die. Besides—" he glanced around him "—this place is a life-changer. Kids need life-changers like this."

"Why'd you come here, Nick?"

Her question must have taken him by surprise because he blinked several times as if gathering his thoughts. "Not to be camp manager, if that's what you're asking."

"Then why?"

"I needed to get away, to refocus. They say working in ministry is a bit like living in a fishbowl. People are watching you all the time, picking apart every little thing you do. After a while, you learn how to go through all the motions that show people you're living the right life. I realized I'd mastered going through the motions, but I want more than that for my life. I needed to focus on what's on the inside."

She nodded. "I can respect that."

"Really? Because I feel like I'm letting everyone down."

"You should never feel guilty about doing the right thing. And you don't have to work in ministry for God to be able to use you."

He smiled. "You always have a way of making the world seem right again, Molly Hamilton."

His words were meant to lift her spirit, but instead she felt herself sagging. She wished she could make herself feel like the world was right again. But with so many things uncertain in her life, she was struggling. Where would she go when her job here ended? Did she really even want to work in a hospital again? Would anyone hire her even?

She shuffled her feet a moment. "I've got to go give some campers their morning medications. They're probably waiting for me now."

Nick nodded, his gaze still latched on hers. She had the impulse to step into his arms and, just for a moment, to feel cared for and protected. Of course, she would never do that. Their past relationship was exactly that—their past. He'd proven himself to be untrustworthy already. She didn't need a repeat reminder.

Finally, he took a step back. "I'll talk to you later then."

Molly hurried down the path before he saw anything else in her gaze. Once in the nurse's station, she sat down for a minute, trying to collect her thoughts. God certainly had a funny way of orchestrating the events in her life. But all things worked for the good of those who were in Christ. Scripture affirmed that, and Molly had chosen to believe it all her life. Now wasn't the time to stop.

A knock sounded at the door. One of the campers had

come to take some anxiety medication. Molly unlocked the medicine cabinet and looked for the girl's prescription. Where was it? She shoved more bottles aside. Molly remembered putting the medication in here. Certainly, she'd just missed seeing it somehow.

She moved more bottles aside, looking carefully at each label. No, the bottle was gone.

"What's wrong, Nurse Molly?"

"I can't find your medicine. You took it yesterday, and I know I put it back in here."

"I saw you lock up the case yourself."

Molly leaned back and drew in a deep breath, praying for clear thought. What could have happened to the medication? She was the only one who had a key to this cabinet and she prided herself on being thorough.

Images from her time at the hospital flashed back into her mind, each memory tightening her muscles until Molly feared they might snap.

She was going to have to tell Nick. But how would he react to the news? Did he know about her past? How would this affect her position at the camp?

TEN

Nick stared at Molly another moment, uncertain that he'd heard her correctly. A moment ago, she'd knocked on his office door then slipped inside, quietly closing the door behind her. He'd known by the look on her face that she had bad news, but he hadn't expected this.

"Drugs are missing?"

Molly nodded, the action tight. "They were there yesterday. Ashley even said she remembers me putting the prescription back into the cabinet after she took her morning dosage. I have no idea what happened to the bottle."

"You locked the cabinet back up?"

"Of course."

"And no one else has the key."

"You're the one who gave me the key. I'm assuming there are no other copies."

He opened his desk drawer and saw a silver key in the corner, just where he'd left it. "There's one other copy, but it's right here." His gaze rose to meet hers. "This isn't good."

"I know." She wrapped her arms over her chest. "I'm flabbergasted."

He hadn't wanted to bring the subject up—not at all. But how could he not, given the circumstances now? He leaned toward her from across the desk. "Molly, is there anything you want to tell me?"

She blinked. "That I want to tell you? What do you mean?"

He suppressed a sigh. She wasn't going to make this easy. "I know about the missing drugs from your last place of employment."

She straightened. "How do you know about that?"

"I checked your employment history. What kind of camp director would I be if I didn't?"

"And you really believe that I stole drugs?"

"I'm not saying that. I'm simply asking you what happened. If you have a problem—"

"A problem? You think I have a drug problem?"

This wasn't going as he'd hoped. Not at all. "That's not what I'm saying, Molly."

"Then what are you saying?"

"I'm simply asking you to tell me the truth."

"I've never lied to you, Nick."

"I'm not saying that you have. But I am saying that the camp is on precarious ground right now. I need to know about your past so I can know how to handle this situation. The last thing either of us wants is for this camp to be shut down, correct?"

Molly nodded slowly. "Of course."

Nick relaxed his shoulders some. "Good, then why don't you tell me what's going on?"

She said nothing for a moment.

"Molly, even if something did happen in your past, it's not going to change the way I think about you. 'Let he who is without sin cast the first stone.' That's not me. I'm not in a place to throw any stones—not that I'd want to anyway."

She buried her face in her hands a moment, as if trying to compose herself. Finally, she heaved in a deep breath and sat up, opening her eyes until her weary gaze met Nick's. "My former boss did make accusations against me. None of them were true, though. He was simply retaliating because I broke up with him. He's used to getting his way and tried to manipulate the situation. The hospital opened an investigation. I voluntarily did a drug test—which was clean, and I also allowed hospital staff to look at my financial records to prove that I hadn't been selling anything. My ex-boyfriend kept persisting—and he was the chief of staff. Finally, I simply agreed to leave. The work environment became too toxic for me to handle any more and I knew I needed a change."

"He really accused you of stealing drugs?"

Molly nodded. "He even tried to come across to everyone else like a hero by offering to pay for me to get treatment. It was despicable."

"I'm sorry."

"Me, too. But that which doesn't kill you only makes you stronger."

"And that's why you came here? To get away from all of that?"

"I need some of that clarity that I had when I was here. Honestly, when I look back on my life, my week I spent here was one of my best weeks ever. I needed to get away from everything else in my life and just focus on getting my heart right."

Nick had always felt a connection with Molly, but it had never felt as strong as at that moment. He wanted to wrap her in his arms and tell her that everything would be okay. He wanted to tell her that he understood, that he'd come back here for the same purpose. But he couldn't do that. It was his responsibility to oversee the camp right now.

He only hoped there was a happy ending to this whole situation.

* * *

The camper's parents called in a new prescription to a local pharmacy, and Molly had left to pick it up. As she disappeared out the door, Nick couldn't stop thinking about everything she'd told him. Her work situation must have been awful. She'd used the word "despicable" when describing the doctor who'd made the accusations against her, and that was a perfect word. Why would someone do something that awful? Had he really thought his manipulation would work? The very thought of it caused anger to surge up Nick's spine.

Another car rumbled up the camp's gravel driveway. Who now?

Nick hurried to the cafeteria door, anxious to know whether his parents or the sheriff had returned. Instead, he saw a luxury sedan with out-of-state license plates. A camper's parent maybe?

Nick watched as a well-groomed man in his early forties exited the vehicle. The dark-haired man approached Nick with a warm smile. Nick braced himself. A lawyer, perhaps? Whoever the man was, Nick had a bad feeling about his presence here.

"Nick White, I presume?" The man offered his hand, a row of perfect white teeth gleaming from a plastered-on smile.

Nick hesitated before returning the man's handshake. "And you are?"

"I'm Dr. Derek Houston. I'm trying to locate someone and I hope you might be able to help."

Derek Houston? Where had Nick heard that name before? "And who is that?"

"Molly Hamilton."

Adrenaline surged through his veins. "You came all

the way out here to the middle of nowhere to find this Molly Hamilton?"

The man's smile dipped slightly. "That's correct. A mutual friend mentioned that she might have come here."

"Must be important to you to talk to her if you drove all the way out here."

The smile disappeared. "She's not answering my calls, so I had no choice but to pay her a visit."

"Maybe she's not answering your calls for a reason."

The man's eyes narrowed. "You don't know who you're dealing with."

"Why don't you tell me then?"

"She has a drug problem that she doesn't want to own up to. I know she seems all sweet and innocent on the outside, but she has some serious problems."

"I'd say the only serious problem she has is you."

Derek's eyes darkened. "I can cause trouble for this camp, you know."

"Don't threaten me, doctor."

The man's features softened for a moment, as if he decided to change his game plan. "Look, this conversation isn't going the way I wanted it to. I really just want to talk to Molly."

"She's not here."

"Do you know when she'll return?"

"Not sure."

"Will you ask her to contact me?"

"I'll give her the message."

"I'm not trying to cause trouble, Mr. White. I simply want to talk to Molly. Despite her issues, she's very special to me, and I screwed things up with her while we were in Maryland." He pointed inside. "I did drive a long way. Do you think I could wait until she returns?"

Nick shook his head. "This is private property, doctor.

Besides, the kids are coming to dinner soon. I'd suggest you leave. If Molly wants to talk to you, she'll contact you."

Nick watched the man leave. He was bad news, the kind of person who could turn his charm on and off in order to manipulate people.

Could he be behind the vandalism at the camp? If the doctor shut the camp down, maybe he thought Molly would go running back to her old job in Maryland. And the bigger question—was the man simply capable of manipulating or was he also capable of violence?

Molly waved as the last car pulled out of the camp, signaling the end of another successful week—despite all the attempts to the contrary.

Molly's pulse had been racing ever since Nick leaned over and whispered that he needed to talk to her earlier. What could it be about? The missing drugs again? She'd thought he believed her when she told what had happened in Maryland. But what if he didn't? What if he'd decided to fire her? She wouldn't blame him. With all the troubles the camp was having, missing drugs, when combined with the accusations against her, certainly didn't help their case.

Three days had passed since the drugs went missing. Yet the thought of what had happened still haunted her. They'd talked to each of the campers and no one seemed to know anything about the drugs. But with only two keys, who else could have gotten into the cabinet without leaving so much as a hint? There were no jimmy marks or broken glass or anything else to indicate someone had forced their way inside.

"Cody's having a campfire complete with s'mores. Want to come?" Nick extended his hand to her.

"Sounds like fun." Without even thinking, she reached

for his hand. His fingers wrapped around hers, sending tingles through every part of her. Once she got to his side, his hand slipped from hers and instead went around her waist.

"I know you don't like the woods," he said as the trees loomed around them.

"No, I don't. Every time I get near them, I think of that night I spent lost in the forest as a child. Some things you just don't ever forget, no matter how hard you try." She shivered even thinking about the experience.

"I've always thought you were brave for even getting as close as you did. Some people would have avoided a camp like this after what you went through."

"I don't want things from my past to hold me back. I just want them to make me stronger."

"You never have held on to your past, Molly. You've always been your own person—determined, strong, wise. I think those are the very traits that have always intimidated my mother."

"I can't imagine how I could intimidate your mom. Most of the people she's surrounded by have her up on a pedestal. Your dad, too."

"That's why she's intimidated. You've always had the ability to see through people, Molly."

"I never saw it like that."

"That's why I broke up with you, Molly. Because I was a coward."

"What do you mean?"

He paused and turned toward her. "I was afraid that you'd see who I really was—someone who was just going through the motions. I could fool almost anyone into believing that I was the perfect Christian when, in truth, I was far from it. I knew as soon as you saw through me that I was going to be the biggest disappointment to you.

I couldn't bear the thought of it. So I broke up with you to spare us both the pain."

"You really thought you were going to disappoint me?"

He grimaced. "I more than thought it. I knew it. You were so strong in your faith. You were one of the most authentic people I'd ever met. You made me realize how much I fell short."

"You're too hard on yourself."

He shook his head and began walking again. "I'm not, Molly. My dad stood in front of the whole church and told everyone that I was going to follow in his footsteps by becoming a chaplain in the Navy. Everyone cried and applauded and said what a good guy I was. I didn't have the willpower to disappoint everyone. So I went to seminary and joined the military."

"What happened over there, Nick?" She grabbed his arm and pulled him to a stop. She gripped his arm, not letting him go. "What brought you back here?"

"I would go into town sometimes when I had some time off. I got to know some of the locals. There were Christians over there who knew that if they got caught they would die for their faith—and they didn't care. In fact, a few of them did die for their faith. I realized what a hypocrite I was. If I were in their shoes, I don't know that I could do the same. I knew I had to make some changes in my life. All of that led me back here. As soon as I finished my stint in the military, I got out and knew I needed to reevaluate my life."

"I think it takes a lot of courage to do that, Nick. Honesty takes courage."

"I appreciate you saying that, but I'm in no way worthy of praise or admiration."

"The beautiful part is that you don't think so. You don't realize what a treasure you are."

"Molly—"

"Come on, guys! We're about to eat all of the chocolate over here!" Cody waved them toward the campfire.

Nick tilted his head. "I guess we'll have to finish this talk later."

"Deal." She dropped her hand from his arm and they walked side by side toward the blazing fire in the distance. A group of Cody's friends were there, laughing and enjoying each other's company. They even joked unknowingly about some of those old scary campfire stories counselors used to tell. Nick and Molly joined in the fun...or at least tried to.

Molly couldn't forget about her earlier conversation with Nick. It pained her to know how much he beat himself up. But the fact that he wanted to be a better person said so much about him. Molly had learned early to accept God's grace but, at the same time, to always push herself to do her best.

Finally, Cody and his friends drifted away. Nick and Molly sat by the fire, its embers crackling and popping. Molly let the flames warm her as she absorbed the sounds of nature around her. Normally being out here in the isolation of the woods would frighten her, but with Nick by her side, she felt safe.

"Derek stopped by this week, Molly."

Molly nearly fell off the bench she perched on. "Derek?"

He nodded. "He said he wanted to talk to you."

"How did he find me here?"

"He said a friend told him."

"I didn't tell anyone where I was going." Her blood went cold. How had he found her?

"I told him to get lost, that this was private property. I've been keeping my eyes open for him since then, but there's been nothing." Nick looked at her. "He threatened to take down the camp, Molly."

She gasped. "He said that?"

"Basically, yes."

"Do you think he's been the one behind everything going on here?"

"I don't know. If he shuts the camp down, maybe he thinks you'd go running back to Maryland, back to him."

"Never. He's trying to control the situation again, and it's not going to work."

"I just wanted to warn you."

"Nick, what if this is all my fault? What if all of these things are happening at the camp because Derek wants to send me a message?"

His hand covered hers. "Don't think like that. Even if it was Derek, everything that's happening wouldn't be your fault."

"No, but if I wasn't here…"

Nick gently turned her chin until she faced him. "If you weren't here, I would have probably lost my mind already. You've been at my side, helping me solve every problem and carry every burden. I don't know what I would have done without you."

Before Molly could respond, a sound in the distance assaulted to her ears. Chainsaws. She looked at the woods, toward the sound. Was someone trying to scare them again?

Before she could question what to do, two figures emerged from the woods—running straight at them.

ELEVEN

Nick grabbed Molly's hand and pulled her to her feet. "Come on!"

Molly didn't have to be told twice. Nick pulled her down the trail back toward the cafeteria. She glanced over her shoulder and saw the men still chasing them. Thankfully, they appeared to have left their chainsaws behind. But something else glinted in their hands—the metal of guns.

A shot whizzed past them, splintering the wood on a nearby tree.

"Are you okay?" Nick yelled, still charging ahead.

Another shot flew past, close enough this time that Molly could smell the smoky acid of the bullet. Her hands trembled from the fear the smell sent coursing through her. "I think so."

He glanced back, but only for a second. "Do you trust me?"

"Trust you?" What was Nick getting at? "Yes, yes, I trust you."

"Then don't let go of my hand." Nick pulled her from the trail into the woods. They wound between trees, over a creek, into the darkness.

Prickles of fear spread over Molly's skin. Each step into

the woods made her breathing grow heavier. Her heart raced faster than a mountain river during flood season.

But she couldn't slow down, couldn't look back. The men were still on their trail, still within shooting distance. Any misstep could mean a bullet into her body, into Nick's body.

She darted around some underbrush, still gripping Nick's hand with all the strength she had in her. As they rounded a briar patch, a branch from a fallen tree sliced into her leg. The pain nearly made her double over.

"Are you okay?" Nick called over his shoulder.

She hobbled forward, trying to ignore the agony ripping through her leg. "We have to keep moving. I'll be fine."

He slowed long enough to run his gaze over her. "You're hurt."

"It's just a cut." Every movement caused her to wince in pain, though. This was a deep cut. As a nurse, she didn't have to see the abrasion to know she'd need some stitches.

"Come on." Nick lifted her into his arms. "Put your arms around my neck and hold on."

She simply nodded, not in the mood to argue. Instead, she tucked her head between Nick's neck and shoulder, grateful for his hard muscles and sure-footedness. She closed her eyes and blocked out the darkness, tried to pretend she was anywhere but the woods.

Nick rounded a cluster of trees and ducked behind them. He sucked in a few deep breaths, still holding Molly close. Silence settled around them for a moment. Finally Nick slowly lowered Molly from his arms and onto the rocky ground.

"You okay?" he mouthed, an arm still around her for support.

She nodded, even though she felt anything but okay. He eased her onto the forest floor, between the protection of several trees. With a finger over his lips to signal silence, Nick peered around the makeshift fortress.

Finally, he lowered himself on the ground beside her and placed a strong hand on her knee. "I think we lost them," he whispered. "Let's stay still a few more minutes just to be sure."

Her heart pounded so hard she felt certain Nick could hear it. Her concern over its loudness only lasted a moment as the searing pain from her cut came to the forefront of her mind. Her cut was deep, deeper than she'd first anticipated.

Her gaze darted around her. Woods. Everywhere stood trees, underbrush, rocks. The forest surrounded them. Each tree might as well be the boogeyman.

Just like when she was a little girl. She'd been lost—and alone—in the wilderness while her mom partied at the campground with a new boyfriend. The search parties hadn't found eight-year-old Molly until the next morning. She'd wedged herself between two trees to ward away the cold and intruders. If it hadn't been for the red outfit she'd been wearing, rescuers might not have found her the next day. She'd been dehydrated and hungry, but otherwise okay.

She closed her eyes, half afraid she might pass out and half praying she would.

Because anything would be better than facing this nightmare around her.

Nick looked beside him, noting that Molly somehow reminded him of a little girl all of the sudden. The pain of her cut, the memories of her childhood seemed to be attacking her now. Her eyes began drooping shut.

"Stay with me, Molly."

She jerked them open, but a glazed look replaced her earlier focus. "I'm here."

Using his index finger, he turned her chin toward him until her gaze locked with his. "Don't look at the woods. Look at me, okay?"

She nodded, but Nick could tell he was losing her. He had to keep her distracted from everything around her— her cut, the woods, the men with guns.

"We're going to be okay, do you understand?"

She nodded again, but her eyes had a paralyzed look to them. He had to get her away from this place, somewhere he could check out her wound and know she was safe. He just needed to buy a few more minutes first.

He gripped her hand and began tapping out a rhythm there. "Do you remember that?"

She nodded. "It was our silent way of communicating so no one else would know." They would give one tap for the letter A, two taps for B, all the way down the alphabet.

"What am I saying now?" He tapped out his message and waited until she grinned.

"You're trying to make me blush."

He shook his head. "No, I mean it. You're beautiful, Molly. Have I ever told you that?"

A slight hint of a smile played on her lips. "It's been awhile."

He swiped a lock of her auburn hair behind her ear and cupped her face with his hand. "You're even more beautiful than before. Time's been good to you, you know."

"You're just saying that so I won't panic." She attempted a laugh, but it came out a sigh.

He caressed her cheek, wanting nothing more than to cover her lips with his. But this wasn't the time or the place. When he kissed her again it wouldn't be at a time she was scared and vulnerable. "I don't want you to panic, but I do mean it when I say you're beautiful, Molly. Even after all of these years, I still look at you and forget about everything else."

Her eyelids fluttered. "Now you really are trying to make me blush."

"It's kind of cute when you blush." He grinned, but let it slip away. "Listen, my grandfather has a hunting cabin not too far from here—it's closer than the rest of the camp. He has a first aid kit there. I'm going to take you there and get a bandage on you. Okay?"

"Okay."

"Do you want me to carry you?"

"Just help me walk."

He stood, confident that the men pursuing them had passed, and held out a hand to Molly. Her eyes squeezed with pain as he pulled her to her feet. He wished there was another way. But every other plan he could think of involved leaving her in the woods while he went to get help. He knew he couldn't do that.

Nick slipped his arm around her waist and waited until she got her balance. "You sure you can do this?"

"No, but I'm willing to give it a shot."

"Okay, here we go then." They stepped forward, Molly hobbling on one leg. Nick tried to help her as much as he could. Finally, after a few steps, they fell into a nice rhythm together.

His grandfather's hunting cabin wasn't far from there. He'd get Molly bandaged up, let her rest a few minutes and then take her back to the camp.

Please, Lord, cover the eyes and ears of the men who were following us. Help them not to hear or see us.

Slowly, surely, they made it to the cabin. Nick carried Molly up the steps to the landing at the front door. He reached for his keys when he noticed the door was open a crack. Cautiously, he pushed at it, watching as it slowly creaked open. He and Molly exchanged a glance. Someone had been here. The question was, who?

He made sure Molly was secure against the porch railing before stepping back toward the door. "Wait here while I check out the inside."

Molly leaned against the rough exterior of the cabin and nodded. Nick stepped inside, his gaze darting about the dark one-room cabin. The place was small enough that it would be hard for anyone to hide out there. Everything appeared still, quiet.

Still on guard, he moved through the darkness to the kitchenette in the corner. Never turning his back on the rest of the cabin, he reached below the sink until he found a propane lantern. The wick flared to life and the cabin came into view. No one was inside, but it was apparent someone had been there.

Molly stepped inside, looking gaunt and pale. Her gaze wandered the space around them. "What happened in here?"

Nick placed the lantern on the kitchen table and shook his head. "I have no idea. The cabin's obviously had visitors."

Food wrappers were on the ground, the mattress leaned against the window, dirty pots littered the stove.

"Someone made themselves at home." Molly picked up an empty bag of potato chips. "Someone very messy made themselves at home."

"Could have been one of the local hunters. They've been using the camp's property for years. My granddad used to hunt before he gave the property over to the camp. Now, if you're hunting this close to the cabins it can be dangerous."

Molly lowered herself into a rickety wooden chair. From the intense look on her face, her cut felt worse.

"Let me get that first aid kit." He rifled around in the bathroom cabinet until he found it. He knew the place was stocked. It had been a provision of his grandfather's will giving the camp this property—the cabin had to remain in case Nick wanted to use it. Nick never hunted, but it was nice to know that there was a place he could go to get away.

He knelt in front of Molly. "Let's see that cut."

Slowly, she rolled up the leg of her jeans. A deep gash sliced through her skin. Nick resisted a flinch as the blood came into sight. Molly had to be in pain from a cut like that.

"You're going to have to take me to the doctor when we get back." Her voice sounded brittle.

Nick knew she was trying to be strong, and he admired her for that. "I'll take you wherever you want when we get back." He pulled out some ointment. "Until then, let's get some antibiotic on this and some butterfly bandages. Okay?"

She nodded and shut her eyes. Nick worked quickly and carefully to bandage up the wound. When he was done, he rocked back on his heels and observed Molly again. He seemed to be doing that a lot lately, and not just when the woman was injured.

He thought he'd put this woman behind him, but the fierceness that welled in his heart when he thought about someone trying to hurt her clearly showed that he still cared about her. It didn't matter, though. A relationship between them would never work. Nick needed freedom from obligations right now, and Molly would never forgive him for abandoning her.

* * *

"You always liked nature, didn't you?" Molly leaned back in the chair and tried to get her thoughts off of the situation at hand.

"Always. I guess I got that from my granddad. He loved nothing more than being out here on his land. I think he saw that same passion in me, which is why he left all of this to me."

"He was the one person who understood you, wasn't he?"

Nick nodded. "He was. I still miss him. He taught me how to build things out of wood, how to cultivate a garden, how to track animals. I used to beg my parents to let me stay with him for the entire summer. Two weeks never seemed like enough."

"What did your dad teach you?"

"How to act like a Christian." He shook his head. "I shouldn't say it like that. My dad's a good man. He just desperately wanted me to follow in his footsteps. I think he'd think of himself as a failure if I didn't."

Molly shook her head. "That's crazy. You have to let your children be who they're created to be."

A slow grin cracked Nick's face. "I like that. That's who I want to be—the person God intended."

Molly brushed Nick's cheek with her thumb. "You're too hard on yourself, Nick."

A rustling sound outside caused them both to straighten. Nick extinguished the lantern and crept toward the door. "Get down."

Molly sank to the floor, praying for safety. Had the men found them? If so, what would they do to them? Simply put a bullet through their head, or would they draw out the process into something much more painful?

"Do you see anything?" Molly whispered.

Nick crouched below the window, peering out through the corner. "Nothing. But I know I heard something."

Molly pushed herself into the wall. "I heard it, too."

He peered out the window a moment. Finally, he sank back down. "I think it was just a wild animal."

"I hope that's all it was."

He turned to her. "Look, Molly. I need to go out to the shed behind this cabin. There's probably a shovel in there. I want to find something that can help you walk, and something to use for added protection, just in case."

She stood. "I'm going with you. You're not leaving me in this cabin all by myself." She felt safer with Nick in the wide open than she felt tucked away by herself.

"Stay close, though."

"Got it."

Pain screamed down her leg as she stood. She gripped Nick's arm, using his steadiness for support. Slowly, they hobbled down the steps. Their feet crunched across dried leaves and cracked twigs lying in their path. Crickets chirping and various other sounds Molly didn't recognize completed the night symphony around them.

"This is an old outhouse that my grandfather converted into a shed," Nick whispered. "I haven't been in here for years—I haven't really had the need to—but I'm pretty sure he should have some tools out here."

Molly nodded, her throat still dry with fear. Though nature didn't hint of any impending attacks or hiding intruders, she still couldn't rest. Letting down her guard would be foolish. For all they knew, their attackers could be at the edge of the woods waiting for them to emerge again. Cody was probably already sleeping and hadn't noticed their absence.

Was this how the previous director had disappeared? Had he been minding his own business when intruders had driven him into the woods? And what had happened if they'd caught him?

Or had Gene simply left? Had he decided camp life wasn't for him and been too much of a coward to let anyone know?

As they got closer to the shed, a foul smell permeated the air.

"It smells like it used to be an outhouse," Molly mumbled.

"I can't argue that."

Nick fumbled for a minute until he found the right key on his key ring. The lock finally clicked and Nick pulled open the door. The stench became stronger, more nauseating, so much so that Molly took a step away.

"An animal must have fallen to the bottom of the place and died. That's the only thing I can imagine would smell that bad."

Molly agreed and let Nick step inside. She wrapped her arms over her chest, suddenly chilly.

Nick suddenly stumbled backward and moaned.

"What is it?"

Nick turned away from the shed, his eyes closed. "It's Gene. He's dead."

TWELVE

Molly looked around the table at the various people gathered at the camp. Nick had called an emergency meeting after the events of last night. Not only were the camp's staff members there—including Cody, Ernie and Molly—but several members of the board of directors and Sheriff Spruill had gathered. They had to make some serious decisions before the next round of campers arrived tomorrow. This meeting just happened to coincide with the board meeting that was supposed to take place today anyway.

"The cause of Gene's death is still undetermined," Sheriff Spruill said. "It's obvious that a wild animal got to him, we just don't know if that happened postmortem or not. The medical examiner is looking at him now, so we should have answers soon."

"This is going to be hitting the newspapers soon and no one will want to send their kids here," Richard Grayson spoke up.

Another board member shook his head. "And someone chased two of our staff with a gun. That's more than a threat. Their lives were in danger. We can't put campers' lives in danger also. We just can't do it."

"None of the campers have been threatened, though." Cody, who'd looked practically comatose earlier, now raised his head from the table. Fire flashed in his eyes. "I'd hate for this place to shut down. Whoever's doing this will win if it does."

"Word's already spreading around town." Ernie, the groundskeeper, stood at the back of the room and looked as if he'd just come from plowing the fields. Dirt and grime were smudged across his face and grass stains decorated his pants. "How will the parents feel if they find out they sent their kids here after all of this violence has been going on?"

Nick ran a hand through his hair and left even more strands than usual standing on end. Molly could tell the situation was getting to him—and rightfully so. She wanted nothing more than to tell him that everything would be all right.

But would it? Would everything be okay?

Finally, Nick straightened his stance at the front of the table and drew in a deep breath. "We have to be honest. I'm not going to let parents leave their children here under the false pretense that nothing's been going on. I refuse to try to cover up the circumstances happening at the camp."

Another board member raised his index finger. "What if we hire some off-duty sheriff's deputies to patrol the camp twenty-four-seven? What if we instigate some new security procedures? And then if a parent still isn't comfortable, we give them a full refund."

"You think parents are going to go for that?" Ernie's eyebrows raised, suspended in doubt.

Nick shrugged and tapped his finger against the table. "They might. Either way, we'd be letting them make the decision. I really don't think the people behind this will hurt the campers. They only seem to be after me and Molly, for some reason. Even last night, I'm not sure they intended to hurt us as much as scare us."

"What about Gene?" someone else asked.

Nick's tapping stopped and he leaned—or was it sagged?—against the table. "We don't know anything for sure."

Sheriff Spruill nodded. "I'm going to have to agree with the board members on this one. I think we need to shut the place down until the people behind these incidents are behind bars. We just can't risk the campers' safety."

Molly's heart sank. The last thing she wanted was for the camp to close. A scandal like this might tarnish the camp's reputation forever. But more than that, she didn't want anyone to be hurt.

They simply had to figure out who was behind this and stop the harrassment as soon as possible, before any more damage was done.

Nick raised his head and nodded. "I agree. That's the only smart thing to do. I couldn't live with myself if something happened to one of our campers. Shutting down the camp is the most responsible thing."

The meeting wrapped up with a promise to convene again in two weeks. In the meantime, the sheriff and his men would continue to investigate the happenings around the camp. At least, Molly tried to reason optimistically, they'd have some time to fix the camp up more.

Molly saw a man, very businesslike in his khakis, button-down shirt and tie, approach Nick after everyone else had cleared away. Molly stayed close by, curious about the conversation.

"I've been checking the books like you asked me to, Nick. There are large sums of money missing."

"Missing?"

The man nodded. "I don't know if Gene was simply a terrible bookkeeper or if something else was going on. But there's a large amount of unaccounted-for funds. I thought you'd want to know."

"Thank you. I appreciate your work." The lines seemed to deepen on Nick's forehead.

When the man walked away, Molly hobbled toward Nick, her leg still aching. She placed her hand on his arm. "You doing okay?"

He nodded solemnly. "I think the decision to shut down the camp is for the best. I'm just afraid this will be the final nail in the coffin, so to speak, when it comes to this camp's survival."

"Things can always turn around," she said, trying to assure him. But even Molly knew things looked grim.

His serious gaze rested on her. "You'll probably want to go ahead and look for another job, Molly."

"Am I fired?"

He shook his head. "No, but we have no way of paying you."

Molly's hands went to her hips. "I'm not going anywhere. As long as I have a place to sleep, I'll be okay."

His gaze still remained serious. "I appreciate your bravado, but you don't have to do that, Molly. I totally understand if you want to leave."

"But I don't. I don't want to leave. I'm not giving up on this camp."

Cody stepped behind them. "Neither am I."

"I'm sticking around, too," Ernie said, appearing from the other room.

Nick's gaze wandered to each of them. "I appreciate your loyalty, guys. But even losing the money for one week of camp will put us so behind that I'm not sure we'll catch up."

Cody shook his head. "I've already talked to my friends

at church. They're organizing a yard sale and bake sale for this week, with all the proceeds going to the camp."

"I've got some savings I can live on, so don't worry about me," Molly said. "And maybe we can get some other churches that support the camp to do some fundraisers."

Cody nodded enthusiastically. "I bet we could organize that. In fact, since I won't have anyone to act as a lifeguard for, I could organize that. I can start making some calls now."

"It could be worth a shot," Ernie agreed.

Nick's gaze still looked weary. "It will be simply amazing if we pull this off."

Molly squeezed his arm. "We can do it."

Nick looked out at the distance in thought before slowly nodding. "Thanks, guys. I don't know what I'd do without you. You're all real lifesavers. I wasn't expecting to be thrust into this position as camp director, but I do know that God works all things for a purpose. I'm going to keep believing that, and I hope you all will, too. This camp isn't going down without a fight."

"That's the spirit!" Molly clapped as if at a pep rally, glad to hear some enthusiasm return to Nick's voice. She knew it had been a hard night for him. He had to call his parents and tell them the news about Gene. Then he drove Molly into town to have her cut looked at. Ten stitches later, they'd returned to the camp and were up for the rest of the night answering questions from the sheriff.

She wished she could say the worst was over. But her gut told her that the worst had only just begun.

Four hours later, Molly, Nick and Cody had called every camper who was supposed to be arriving tomorrow and informed them of the change of plans. Reactions had ranged from disbelief to disappointment to outrage.

The staff had assured everyone that their money would be refunded and that the whole ordeal would hopefully be cleared up very soon.

When they were done, Cody met some of his friends from church who'd decided to pitch in, buy some paint and give the cabins a fresh coat. Nick had to admire the group for their tightness, loyalty and enthusiasm. Molly disappeared to the nurse's station to see if anything needed to be restocked. And Nick sat in his office, staring at a blank computer screen.

For a moment earlier today, he'd actually entertained the idea of leaving the camp permanently. After all, this place had been one big headache since he'd arrived and being director here was not even on his long-range agenda. But then everyone had stepped up with such enthusiasm. He'd known at that moment that if he were to leave, it would be one of his biggest regrets. Nick needed to stand behind the camp with the same loyalty his staff members had.

But Gene... His cousin's image flashed into his mind. What had happened to his cousin? Had a wild animal attacked him? Nick's gut told him that wasn't what happened. Had the men from the woods killed him? Nick didn't want to believe that to be true. He wanted to think the threats were empty. Could it have been a terrible accident? A heart attack? Again, Nick shook his head. He had to stop playing this guessing game.

A soft knock sounded at his door and a moment later Molly peeked her head inside. "Bad time?"

He shook his head, his mood already lighter. "Never a bad time to see you."

A hesitant smile crossed her face as she lowered herself into a chair across from him. "As I was sorting through our medical supplies, I started thinking about this whole situation, Nick," she started. "All of the threats seem to be centered on the woods. We've mentioned hunters who want to use the property. We've mentioned someone wanting to buy the land for a factory. But what if someone was doing something illegal on the land?"

"What do you mean?"

She shrugged. "I mean, what if someone is growing marijuana or something? I've heard of things like that happening, and the land the camp owns would be a perfect place to hide a crop like that because the area is so remote."

He tilted his head in contemplation. "I never thought of that."

She shrugged again. "Maybe I'm off base. But you have been clearing some hiking paths. What if those paths are getting closer and closer to whatever's going on? Maybe that's why someone wants this property or why they want to run you off of this property—before you figure out what's going on."

"That's a thought, Molly. The problem is that we have so many acres here. How will we know what's going on with the property? It would take forever to comb the entire area."

"A flyover, maybe? I don't know. I hadn't thought that far ahead. I was just down in the nurse's station thinking about those drugs that went missing. My mind went from there."

"I'll talk to the sheriff. Maybe we can figure something out."

Molly stood. "We've got to get to the bottom of this somehow."

"*We?* You mean, the sheriff."

"Of course." She paused and then sat back down. "Okay, I admit that it's hard for me to sit back and do nothing. I want to be out there solving this thing. I can't stand to think about the camp being shut down for the rest of the summer."

"I don't want to think about that, either. But even more than that, I don't want to think about something happening to you." The very thought of it made his stomach clench.

Footsteps coming down the wood floor of the hallway quieted them. Nick's parents appeared in the doorway. Mrs. White's scowl immediately fell on Molly. Molly excused herself. It was probably a good thing that she wouldn't be around for any more of the drama that seemed to happen when his parents were around lately.

His mom and dad shuffled into the close quarters and closed the door. They stood awkwardly in front of his desk.

Nick pointed to the chairs. "Care to have a seat?"

His parents perched on the edge of the faded chairs, their postures stiff and uncomfortable. Nick's dad spoke first. "We've heard from Richard about everything happening here, son. We don't like it. And your aunt Emma Jean is devastated over the news of Gene. He was her only son. I hate to say it but, this camp is bad news."

The unseen weight on Nick's shoulders suddenly felt heavier. "I'm in charge of things around here now. I have to see this through to completion. I can't let all of the good things that take place here disappear forever."

"You're being foolhardy." His mother's knuckles whitened as she grasped the purse in her lap. "We raised you better than this."

"You raised me to be responsible, to not give up, to work hard. That's exactly what I'm doing."

His mother's voice softened. "You had so much potential, Nicholas. Why'd you throw it all away?"

Nick shook his head, certain that his mother would never see this situation his way. "I didn't throw it away,

Mom. I just realized I had to make some changes in my life, that it couldn't keep on going the way it was."

"What was so wrong with being a chaplain?" His dad blinked back disappointment. "You had a bright career ahead of you. Everyone I talked to said so."

"Being a chaplain was never my true calling. I'm glad I did it while I did. I saw lives changed. I know God used me. But it was time for me to take a step back."

His dad's chin hardened. "I see."

Silence stretched between them. Finally, his mom cleared her throat. "Gene's funeral will be this week. You will be there, won't you?"

"Of course I'll be there."

She gave a curt nod. "And you'll be cautious while staying here at the camp?"

"Mom, I served over in Iraq. I think I can handle Camp Hope Springs."

The first touch of a smile passed over his mother's features. As quickly as it appeared, it vanished. She held her head high and nodded instead. "Very well. There's one more thing I wanted to talk to you about."

Nick braced himself, sure that he didn't want to hear what she had to say.

Molly sat outside the cafeteria, enjoying the quiet for a moment. What were Nick's parents doing here? Would they ever accept Molly? Even now with her and Nick just being friends they seemed to shun her. His parents were overbearing. Molly knew on a logical level that his parents, deep down, loved him more than anything. They just had a funny way of showing it sometimes.

Her thoughts drifted to yesterday. What had gone on between her and Nick? Every time Molly turned around, he seemed to be flirting with her. Certainly he wasn't playing with the idea of a romance flaring between them again…was he? Because that would never happen.

Nick had broken her heart once before. She couldn't risk that again. She couldn't risk struggling with feeling like she wasn't good enough. She couldn't face feeling abandoned again. It's why she'd worked so hard to be self-sufficient in her life, to show everyone that she could handle herself despite her circumstances. A blast from her past wasn't going to change that now.

So why did she constantly entertain the idea of being with Nick again? And why did she always want to be near him?

She knew the answer. Her feelings for Nick had really never died, despite the pain he'd caused. But feelings didn't matter. It was what she did with her feelings that counted. Acting on her feelings now would only lead to heartache further down the road.

What had he said yesterday? That he'd broken up with her out of fear that she'd see the real him? Could that be the truth? Had he really not ended things because he'd felt *she* wasn't good enough?

He seemed to have grown since then into a man who was comfortable in his own skin, who was comfortable with admitting his mistakes and failures and weaknesses. And Molly found that incredibly attractive.

At the center of it, Nick had a heart that sought to help others and to follow God. That was the most attractive thing.

The sheriff pulled up, his visits seemingly becoming part of his daily routine.

"How's it going, Sheriff Spruill?"

"I want to send some of my men out to search for any evidence we may have missed last night."

"I'm sure that's fine."

"I have a couple of questions for Nick about his grandfather's cabin. Is he around?"

"Let me get him for you."

Molly hurried upstairs and raised her hand to knock on his door when the conversation on the other side caught her attention. She paused, hand in air, and stepped closer to the door.

"The girl's always been a bad influence on you, Nicholas," his mother's voice rang out.

"Mom—"

"Just hear me out," she insisted. "You're going to regret it if you change your life's course for her. She may be pleasing to the eye but in the long run she'll only bring you down. The apple doesn't fall far from the tree. She doesn't fit into our family and nothing will ever change that."

Silence responded. Nick didn't argue or defend her. Maybe he'd finally seen the light. Maybe, deep inside, he realized the truth of his parents' words. Maybe he'd always realized the truth, he'd just been in denial.

Tears pricked Molly's eyes as Mrs. White's words slammed into her heart. Molly knew the truth—she knew she'd risen above her upbringing, that she was a child of God and that her self-esteem could be found in Him. Despite that, sadness pressed down on her chest.

Her throat burning with emotion, she fled. The sheriff would have to come up here and find Nick himself because Molly wasn't in the mood to face Nick's parents right now. She disappeared into the nurse's station and closed the door, needing a moment to herself.

All these years she'd been holding out for God's best for her life and now, in an instant, she felt like she wasn't worth God's best. Her mind knew the truth, but her heart wasn't convinced yet. She'd be civil toward Nick, she decided. But she had to put some distance between them. Her heart couldn't handle another rejection from Nick.

The sound of someone pounding down the steps rattled the ceiling above her. Nick's parents must be leaving. She wondered if they'd made peace. She wondered if Nick had finally seen their way of thinking. Would he even tell her about their conversation?

Cody's voice broke the silence. Molly opened the door to her quarters, the urgency of his tone tightening her muscles. She stepped into the cafeteria and saw Cody with the sheriff and Nick. What had happened now?

"What's wrong, Cody?" Molly stepped toward him.

"Laura's gone. No one's seen her for two hours now."

Molly closed her eyes. No, not Laura. The counselor still had so much of her life ahead of her...

"Where was the last place you saw her?" Nick asked.

Cody swallowed so hard that his Adam's apple jerked up and down. "Walking toward the woods."

THIRTEEN

"You should have stayed at the cafeteria, Molly. I can tell your leg hurts."

Molly pushed ahead, ignoring the ache. "I want to help look for Laura."

"Aside from your injury, you hate the woods."

"I hate the woods, but I have priorities. I can't stand the thought of her being lost out there...or even worse."

Nick placed his hand on the small of Molly's back as they continued deeper into the forest. Everyone at the camp and several sheriff's deputies had divided into search teams. No one was to go into the woods alone, though. Nick knew as soon as Molly had volunteered to help that he wasn't letting her out of his sight.

He had to admire her decision to venture into the forest again, especially considering how terrified she was. But Molly had always had the ability to separate from her emotions and do the right thing.

Her eyes had had a distant look to them since she'd emerged from her quarters earlier. What was that about? Had she gotten another message from Derek? Was she second-guessing her decision to stay here? Something appeared to have gotten her down.

She didn't seem in the mood to talk, so instead Nick let

silence fall between them. As the trail narrowed, Nick's thoughts went to his visit with his parents. Their talk hadn't gone so well. He respected his parents and loved them, but setting up boundaries proved difficult. Would his parents ever accept that he was his own man? Sometimes he thought they feared disappointing their congregation more than they cared about Nick's happiness.

Anger still burned in him when he remembered the way they'd spoken about Molly. Molly didn't fit into their perfect little vision they had for his future. After a moment of composing himself, he'd tried to explain to them that their vision for his future wasn't his vision. They'd never given Molly a chance.

He remembered the first time he'd brought her home to meet his folks. Things had started well. Then they began asking about her background. What do your parents do for a living? they'd questioned. Molly had told them that her dad left when she was a toddler, and her mom worked as a waitress at a diner in town. They lived in an apartment in the not-so-good part of town—the only place they could afford. Molly's past had included drinking and partying before she found Jesus. And she had never been willing to accept things at face value or simply because that was the way they'd always been done. She thought for herself, in short.

"Is everything okay, Molly?"

"I just have a lot on my mind."

"Anything you want to talk about?"

"Not particularly." She kept marching forward without so much a glance back.

Just yesterday, it seemed like they'd been on track to starting a relationship again. What had happened to make her change her mind? Had Nick done something to upset her?

"Do you think Laura wandered into the woods, Nick?"

At least she was talking to him. "I'm not sure. Her car is still at the camp, so we know she didn't leave. Cody said she'd gotten irritated with some of the guys and taken a walk to cool off some. I just hope she didn't get lost out here."

Nick saw Molly shiver. "Me, too."

Around the trail they hiked, the woods fully immersed them. Everywhere they looked there were trees and underbrush and not a sign of life outside of nature. To Nick, this place was heaven, a refuge. He wished the same were true for Molly. He wished she would let him take her hand or give him a hug. But Nick didn't dare try that now, not until he got to the bottom of her sudden mood change.

"Is this one of the paths you cleared?"

"Yeah, I started to do that before I found out I was camp director."

"You've always loved camping, backpacking, being out in nature, haven't you?"

"There's nowhere else I feel closer to God. That's one of the reasons I came back to Camp Hope Springs when I got out of the military. I knew this was the perfect place to reexamine my relationship with God."

She shoved a branch out of the way. "How's that worked out for you?"

"I thought it would be my time alone that made me feel closer to God, but instead it's been the opposite. Seeing all of these young people getting excited about their faith has renewed my excitement."

"That's great, Nick. I'm glad that worked out for you."

He grabbed her arm until she stopped and turned toward him. "Molly, what's going on inside that head of yours? I want to help."

Her gaze searched his for another moment before she

finally licked her lips. "I heard what your mom said, Nick. I was coming to tell you the sheriff had arrived, but I overheard your conversation with your parents, instead."

His heart sunk. "Molly, I'm sorry you had to hear that. Just because my parents feel like that doesn't mean that I do. I think what my mom said was despicable. I'm so sorry that she hurt you."

"I don't like feeling that I'm so weak that she has that power over me."

"Even the strongest person can crumble under harsh, undeserved criticism like that. What can I do to make things better?"

Molly looked in the distance for a moment before shaking her head. "Nothing. You didn't do anything wrong."

He didn't know what else to say to her. He wanted to take away her hurt, but was uncertain how to do so. So instead they began walking silently again.

Maybe he should have taken her into his arms? Kissed away her insecurities? Just held her? He didn't know, and not knowing made him feel a bit like a louse.

He sighed and moved forward. He had to think about Laura right now. That was the only thing that might help him keep his sanity.

Molly had hoped that Nick didn't share his mother's feelings. But based on his reaction, he did.

He didn't try to comfort her. He'd only said, *I'm sorry.*

What had she wanted? For him to proclaim his feelings for the world to hear?

Of course not.

She cleared her burning throat. "Are there springs around here? Is that where the camp got its name?"

"No, actually, there aren't. My grandfather named the camp. He chose the name because he believed you could always bounce back from whatever circumstance life handed you. He always said that hope could spring from the direst of situations."

She nodded. "I like that. I can't believe I never heard that explanation before."

"My grandfather really lived that out, too. He grew up with nothing, but he worked hard and was able to purchase this property. He faced other obstacles—his wife died not long after my father was born, he lost two fingers in an auto accident, he eventually began having heart problems. But he always found the good in the bad."

"I think I would have liked your grandfather."

"I think you would have, too."

The trail came to an end, and Molly sucked in a breath. What now?

Nick stopped behind her, nearly colliding with her.

"Do we turn around and go back?"

He glanced at his watch. "We still have an hour and half before we meet back with everyone. We could go a little farther, if you're up for it."

The thought of leaving the trail made her throat go dry. But she nodded. "You're not going to get us lost, are you?"

"I wouldn't do that to you." He pointed in the distance. "It looks like someone has come this way recently. You can tell by the way the underbrush is trampled."

Molly's pulse quickened. "Laura?"

"Could be."

Or it could be from one of the men who'd been terrifying anyone around these woods lately. Molly knew it was a chance they had to take. She couldn't bear the thought of Laura being lost out here. The girl had come across as a bit flighty, the kind who didn't think through things before acting out.

"It's a little rocky right here. Let me help you." Nick

scrambled in front of her as the trail began to slope downward toward a dried creek bed.

Molly slipped her hand into Nick's and scolded herself for the electricity she felt jolt through her at his touch. She wanted to get Nick out of her mind, to forget the idea that they could ever be together. Her body seemed to be reacting differently, though.

The ground slipped from beneath her and she felt herself falling, gravity pulling her downward. Nick's strong arms encircled her before she hit the ground. Just his nearness caused her pulse to quicken uncontrollably.

"Whoa," Nick mumbled as he pulled her up. "Easy does it."

She quickly righted herself, scolding herself for enjoying her closeness to Nick. *Get some distance,* she reminded herself. Distance. She brushed some dirt from her shorts. "Thanks."

"Anytime." He released her and Molly instantly missed the feeling of his arms around her.

Ahead, more sunlight filtered in through the forest, as if the density of the trees eased some.

"What's up ahead?"

Nick shrugged. "Not sure. Let's go find out."

Could they have found the part of the forest where trees had been cleared and some illegal substance was being grown? Was her theory correct?

They climbed over downed trees and through thick underbrush, heading toward the area. Finally, they reached the edge of the clearing. They both stopped and stared.

It appeared that six large trees had been cut down. From the pale color of the wood on the stumps, the trees had been cut recently. A makeshift road jutted from the other side of the area, perhaps where the trees had been pulled from the property?

"What do you think of this?" Molly asked, still perplexed.

"I'm not sure. Why is someone clearing this land—land that doesn't belong to them?"

"Good question. Are they planning to build something? Grow something? Hide something back here in the woods?"

"I have no idea." Nick stood with his hand on his hips, looking at the find before them and shaking his head. "This isn't their property to do anything with. But now the chainsaws make sense. They weren't just using them to scare us. Someone was using them to cut down trees."

"I wonder where that road leads."

"I intend on finding out—just not right now. We've got to get back to the camp before everyone gets worried. We're going to have to hurry to make it on time."

Molly's leg was beginning to ache from walking so much, but she didn't want her discomfort to show. Instead she nodded, dreading the walk back.

Suddenly, Nick stopped in front of her. She nearly collided with his back. What did he see? Laura? One of the men terrorizing the camp? "What is it, Nick?"

Nick remained frozen. "Don't move."

Molly peered around him. Her skin crawled when she saw a snake directly in their path, its body coiled and fangs bared.

"That's a cottonmouth snake, and she doesn't look too happy."

Nick watched as the snake showed its legendary white mouth to them, its fangs flashing in all their glory. One bite from the venomous snake could kill someone. He knew the critter was probably just as afraid of them as they were of it, but they still had to be cautious. Frightened animals responded defensively sometimes.

Molly gripped his arm but otherwise froze behind him.

"If we don't bother the snake, it shouldn't bother us," he mumbled, his eyes never leaving the venomous creature.

"You sure about that?"

"Positive." Ninety-nine percent positive, at least.

He stared at the creature, waiting to see its next move. Would it lunge toward them? Would it continue to block their path until they found another way? And if they did venture off the path, would they stumble into the snake's nest, buried deep in the underbrush?

Finally, the cottonmouth recoiled. The creature slithered away into a nearby bush. Nick released his breath before turning toward Molly. Based on the way her hands fluttered and her eyes darted, she was scared.

"I've got to get out of these woods," she mumbled.

For the rest of their walk, they each seemed lost in their own thoughts, and Nick didn't have the energy at the moment to translate the silence. Was it a good thing? Or was Molly still hanging on to her hurts? Were those hurts irreparable? Did they have any hope for a future together? Perhaps God had brought Molly back into his life for closure. He tried to tell himself that he'd be happy with only her friendship—and, on one level, he would be satisfied with that. But suddenly he was beginning to think that he might want to be more than friends. Being around her these past few weeks made him realize what he was missing out on.

He turned his thoughts to the other matters at hand. They hadn't located Laura, but Nick sure hoped that someone had and that the girl was okay. Every year they seemed to have at least one camper or staff member who liked to wander into the woods and got turned around. They'd never lost anyone yet. He hoped that record would stand, but as he thought about everything happening at the camp lately, he feared the worst.

As his feet pounded the dirt trail, his thoughts returned to the missing trees. He wanted to get to the bottom of whatever was going on in these woods. His mind raced through different possibilities, but none of them made sense, at least not given the information he had.

Certainly a conservation group wouldn't cut down trees. Nor would hunters, who valued trees for their protection while searching for game. Wendell wouldn't be foolish enough to begin clearing trees from land he didn't own for a factory he had no right to build. So who did that leave? Could someone have cut down the trees to grow drugs out here? Certainly they could have found other locations that would have been more hospitable to growing the illegal plants. Nothing made sense. He only knew that these incidents were escalating, and he feared where that might lead.

Finally, they emerged from the wilderness. Molly immediately seemed to relax. Her shoulders sloped some, her arms didn't look so tight.

"Thanks for coming with me, Molly," he said. "You're a real trooper."

"I just hope Laura's okay."

Nick spotted a large group gathered by the cafeteria. He pushed ahead to see what was going on. He parted the college-aged students and saw a teary-eyed Laura sitting in the middle of the gathering.

Laura looked up at him, her entire face blotchy and wet. "I'm so sorry. I didn't mean to cause all of this trouble. I just wanted a moment alone. I had no idea…"

"What happened?" Nick knelt down beside her.

She sniffled. "I went down to the old campfire for a mo-

ment. When I came back up here, I found out that search
parties had gone out looking for me. I'm so sorry, Nick."

"Are you okay?"

She nodded, her chin trembling.

"That's all I care about right now. That's the important
thing." Nick squeezed her shoulder and handed her a bottle
of water. "Drink up."

He stood, one burden lifted. Now he had to find the
sheriff and tell him what they'd discovered.

After most of the crowds had dispersed and Nick left
with the sheriff, Molly wandered inside. She spotted Laura
sitting at a cafeteria table apart from the rest of the people
who had lingered, still obviously upset from the events
from earlier today. Molly slid into a chair next to her. She
softly placed her hand on the girl's shoulder.

"Do you want to talk about it?"

Laura shrugged and balled up a tissue. "I feel so foolish."

"Why?"

The girl wiped at her tears. "I thought Cody liked me.
We've been flirting for the past few months, and I thought
a relationship was just around the corner. But then someone told me he's actually dating someone he met here at
the camp."

"Someone he met here?" *Who would that be?* Molly
wondered.

"A camper, I guess." Laura shrugged and sniffled again.
"I just found out and I wanted to let the news sink in, so
I decided to take a walk. I should have told someone. I
know I should have."

"You were hoping Cody would come after you, weren't
you?"

Her chin trembled again. "I guess. Isn't that stupid? Why would I act that way to get a guy's attention?"

"Guys can make girls go a little crazy sometimes. And, if it makes you feel better, Cody was really worried about you."

Laura tossed a balled up tissue on the table. "I just need to get over him."

Molly offered a half smile, half frown. "I know the feeling."

Laura turned toward her. "How do you know the feeling? You have Nick. Even for an old guy, he's pretty cute."

Molly blinked, both from the insinuation that she *had* Nick and that twenty-eight was old. "I don't *have* Nick. We're just friends, Laura. Nothing more."

"Anyone can see that you're more than friends, Molly." Laura's bloodshot eyes took on a no-nonsense look that was so intense Molly almost laughed. Almost.

"Sometimes things aren't what they seem."

"You guys seem perfect together."

Molly's throat felt dry. "There's no such thing as perfect."

"What's not perfect about the two of you together? You're both nice, attractive, you love God. Sounds perfect to me."

"Thanks for the vote of confidence. But relationships are a little more complicated than that."

"Tell me about it." Laura stood. "I should go back home and end this misery. Maybe I'll move, go out of state, do something to make the pain of rejection more bearable."

"How about you just give it time?" But Molly knew that time didn't always do the trick, either. She didn't mention that, though. No need to add to the drama of young love any more than she had to.

The cafeteria door opened and both Laura and Molly

snapped their heads toward the sound. Molly's stomach sank when she spotted Derek grinning in the doorway.

"Who's that?" Laura mumbled.

Molly sighed. "No one."

"Wait, you have two guys after you? How fair is that?"

Molly ignored Laura as she stepped toward Derek. "What are you doing here?"

"I never thought I'd catch you here. You're a hard woman to locate."

"How'd you find me here?"

He shrugged and brushed a fly from his shoulder. "The camp director called one of my friends at the hospital to report that you were here. My friend let me know about the call. Lucky for me, huh?"

Nick had called to notify the hospital of her whereabouts? Had he not believed what she'd told him?

"Nick reported me?"

"He didn't want a drug thief working for him, especially not after the medications went missing from your care. It was the only responsible thing to do."

Hurt crashed into her heart. She'd known that Nick did a background check on her. But how could he betray her like this? He could have at least told her what he'd done. Or should she even trust Derek? He'd proven himself manipulative before. Still, a touch of doubt nagged at her.

"You know I'm not a drug thief. You were the one who implicated me and threatened me and tried to manipulate the situation in order that I would run back into your arms."

His lips twitched. "Sure, I know you're not a drug thief. I'm sure I could convince everyone else, if you'd let me."

"What are you doing here, Derek?"

His eyes sparkled. "I want to talk to you about coming back to work at the hospital. I want to make things right."

"I'm never going back there, Derek."

"I miss you."

"The answer is still no. I've closed that chapter of my life. It's done. I'm here now."

"If this is about the drug allegations—"

Molly's gaze cut around the room to where everyone appeared to be listening now. "Do not bring that up."

"Perhaps you'd like to chat in my car then, somewhere more private?" The smug sound of his voice made it apparent that his words had the desired effect.

Anger welled inside Molly. Derek wasn't dangerous, so she wasn't afraid to be alone with him, she simply had no desire to. Still, she didn't want all the impressionable college-aged kids around here to overhear this conversation. Finally, she nodded. "Fine, I'll talk to you in private, but, for the record, I don't appreciate you coming here."

He nodded and started toward his car, waiting a beat for her to catch up with him. "Is there anywhere we could get some coffee?"

"I'm not going anywhere with you. If we talk, we talk here."

"Fine then. We talk here."

She folded her arms over her chest. Why couldn't Derek just leave her alone? She'd known that he was used to getting what he wanted, but did he really have to be this persistent? Did he really think he had any chance with Molly after the drug theft allegations he'd issued against her? They'd just been another way of trying to manipulate her.

She would not make the same decisions her mother did. She wouldn't turn to men as a way to fill the voids in her life. She wouldn't make stupid decisions just so she could feel someone's arms around her. She'd made that mistake once with Derek, but she wouldn't make it again.

"You're looking good, Molly," he said. "The sun and fresh air has been good for you, I see."

"Being away from you has been good for me."

"Come now, is that really necessary? I thought we had something good between us." He tilted his head toward her in a way that Molly was sure he intended to look charming.

"You thought that you trying to ruin my life equated to something good between us?"

He laughed slowly, the sound filled with cockiness. "I wasn't trying to ruin your life, dear. I was simply trying to get you to see how good we'd be together. You need some persuasion."

"You're a doctor. You're supposed to heal. Instead, you just corrupt those around you. It's a disgrace."

His smile slipped, but only for a moment. "You've never minced words, have you?"

"Not when I'm speaking the truth."

"Just one more thing to love about you."

Molly looked away, taking a deep breath as she tried to compose herself. Finally she dragged her eyes back up to meet Derek's. "Derek, why are you really here?"

"I told you. I want to take you back to Maryland with me."

"Back to the place where everyone thinks I stole drugs? Even if I've been cleared, you know some people will always doubt my innocence."

He shrugged, as if he didn't have a care or concern in the world. "I've informed everyone that your drug test came back clean and you're no longer under investigation. My influence and opinion go a long way."

"Have you?" Why did she doubt his words? Even if they were true, he'd done so not out of the goodness of his heart, but as a way to manipulate the situation.

"I told you I could make it go away."

"Derek, there are a ton of women out there who would love to be with a handsome doctor. Why are you focused on me?"

He reached over to touch her arm, but she jerked away. His arm fell to his side. "I just want you to see that we'd be perfect together."

"Hardly. We share none of the same values."

He shrugged again. "Minor detail."

Molly clamped her mouth shut. "We're done, Derek. You've just proven to me over and over again that men aren't trustworthy."

She turned on her heel and stomped back to her room, reminded once again by how easily people could be blinded by their weaknesses.

FOURTEEN

"So you're going to call your friend with the forestry extension office?" Nick clarified with the sheriff as they made their way down the trail back toward the camp.

"I'll see if he can come out this week. I just want him to have a look at those trees, see if there's any significance to what kind they are or the way they were cut. There's no evidence that anything else has been planted in that area—not yet at least. Of course, there are other areas of the camp's property that we need to look at."

"How are you going to do that?"

"I'm going to see if I can fly over using one of the local crop-dusting planes. That would be the easiest and most time-efficient way."

"I agree. Maybe you'll see something from up there that we can't see from down here."

"Absolutely. That's my hope."

Just as they emerged from the woods, Nick spotted the taillights of a black luxury sedan heading away from the camp. Who was that? Nick realized it was that doctor who had come looking for Molly last week. Why had he come back to the camp?

Nick's first thought was Molly. He hoped the doctor hadn't upset her. He wanted nothing more than to rush toward the cafeteria and find her. But first he had to wrap up things with the sheriff.

The sheriff turned to him as they stepped onto the gravel trail leading toward the cafeteria. "I'll file the report. I know you're ready to put all of this behind you."

"Been ready."

The sheriff looked in the distance before slowly nodding. "I think it was a smart thing to cancel camp until we find out what's going on here. We don't usually see incidents like this out here."

"Something shady is going on, that's for sure. I appreciate all of your efforts, Sheriff." Nick shook the sheriff's hand as they went their separate ways.

As soon as the sheriff disappeared into his cruiser, Nick hurried toward the cafeteria. He hoped he wouldn't find Molly there, upset over the doctor's visit. As the screen door slapped shut behind him, his gaze roamed the large room. Several of the college kids, including Cody and Laura, sat around at the tables talking. Molly was nowhere in sight, though.

Nick approached Laura, who'd been watching him since he walked in. "Do you know where Molly is?"

"She's in her room. She didn't look very happy."

"What happened?"

Laura shrugged, her eyes still red-rimmed. "Some man came and they started arguing. Then Molly stormed inside and I haven't seen her since. The man stayed around for a few more minutes until he finally left."

Nick clamped his mouth shut. Molly could talk to whomever she wanted, he realized. So why did he feel a surge of jealousy and protectiveness rush through him?

He stomped down the hallway and knocked at her door. A moment later, the door opened and a red-eyed Molly stood there.

"What's wrong? Did that man do something to you?"

She blinked. "That man?"

"The doctor."

She stared at him and shook her head. "No, he's gone. Hopefully for good."

Relief flooded through Nick. He wanted to reach out to her, but stopped himself. "Are you okay?"

"I'll be fine, Nick."

"I want to help."

She shook her head. "There's nothing you can do. Nothing at all."

His heart seemed to stop. Fixing things was what he did best. Why wouldn't Molly let him inside?

He bit his lip. Is this what others felt around him? That there were walls that he wouldn't let them past?

Finally, he nodded. "I'm here if you need me."

She nodded, but her eyes looked listless. "Good night, Nick."

Molly avoided Nick for the rest of the week.

Just when Molly thought Nick respected her and was different from the other men who'd been in her life, she found out that he'd been snooping into her background. He didn't trust her at all, did he? Nothing had changed since they'd broken up.

And that thought made her heart heavy.

She sat in the back of The Hill, where Gene's funeral was being held. The sheriff had informed them this week that the official cause of death had been blunt force trauma to the head and the case went from missing persons to homicide. There were no suspects in his death, however.

Molly watched as Nick fidgeted beside his mom at the front of the room. Despite her anger toward him, all she wanted at the moment was to tell him that everything would be okay. But she couldn't do that. Not only was Nick off-limits, but the question remained: *Would* everything be okay? Someone had murdered Gene. The same person had most likely chased Nick and Molly through the woods. The camp was on the verge of being shut down. Everything didn't seem all right by any stretch of the imagination.

Poor Gene. She still remembered the sight of his dead body, the smell of death. No one deserved to die like that. And why? Why had someone killed Gene? As a means to shut down the camp? Had he discovered the downed trees? Or was he involved somehow?

The funeral was a blur for Molly. Afterward, attendees gathered to chat quietly before heading to the graveside service. Molly hovered close to Cody and his friends, trying not to make the day any harder on Nick by upsetting his family with her presence.

"Molly Hamilton?"

Molly jerked her head up and saw a small woman, probably Molly's age, standing at her side. She looked vaguely familiar. "That's me."

"It's Teresa Neville. We went to camp together way back when."

Teresa Neville. Molly remembered now. The woman had been a shy, slightly mousy girl who'd desperately needed a friend. "Teresa, how are you? It's been a long time."

"I'm fine." She wrung her hands together. "Can you believe I'm still here? Almost everyone from our camp days is gone now."

"The area's a good place to be, though, isn't it? Nick and I are back in the area also."

Her gaze cut to Nick. "You and Nick...?"

Molly shook her head. "No, I didn't mean it that way. We're just working together at the camp. That's it."

"Out of all the couples I knew who dated in high school, I always thought you two would be the ones who made it. You guys were just perfect together."

"Life sometimes turns out differently than what one might expect."

She laughed. "I still remember when the two of you sang that Sonny and Cher song at the talent show. You two were hilarious."

"You mean terrible." Molly smiled at the memory of being carefree and goofy and in love. Her smile slipped, replaced with grief over the loss of what could have been.

"Then we crowned you both the unofficial king and queen of Camp Hope Springs at the camp banquet at the end of the week."

"You even made crowns out of aluminum foil." Molly chuckled. "I have great memories of that week."

"I do, too, thanks to you. I remember I wanted to go home after the first day. But you reached out to me and encouraged me to stick it out. I don't think I ever thanked you for that."

"There's no need for thanks. Sometimes people just need a little encouragement."

Teresa's face turned serious. "It's just terrible about Gene, isn't it?" She lowered her voice. "I heard what happened. Not to speak ill of the dead."

"What did you hear?"

She stepped closer. "Not to spread gossip, but rumor has it that he'd done a secret deal with Wendell to let him rent the land—he knew he couldn't sell it. Wendell gave him a payment but then Gene changed his mind, said he couldn't do it. Trouble is that Gene had already spent the money."

"How do you know all of this, Teresa?"

She blushed. "Gene and I went on a few dates."

Molly digested the new information. Did Gene get himself in trouble financially? Did it get him killed? And was someone still terrorizing the camp as a way of getting even?

As Molly chewed on the thought, she glanced over at Nick's dad. Sweat covered the man's forehead and his eyes looked glazed. Immediately, Molly's instincts went on alert. She excused herself from her conversation with Teresa.

"Mr. White, are you okay? You're looking a little pale."

"Molly." It almost looked like he tried to smile for a moment before his hand went to his chest. "Not feeling... too great." Suddenly, the man slumped over, sending a paper fluttering to the ground. Molly caught him before he hit the floor.

"Nick! Help me!"

Nick looked over, concern flashing in his eyes as he rushed to them. Mrs. White glanced up and screamed at the same moment.

Molly found Mr. White's pulse. It was barely there.

And then it was gone.

"He's having a heart attack. Get him on the floor. Lay him down. We've got to start CPR."

Nick lowered his father onto the floor of the multipurpose room. Mrs. White fell to her knees beside him, weeping as a crowd gathered around them.

Molly got on her knees and positioned herself to begin chest compressions.

"Someone call 9-1-1," Molly shouted. "There's an automated external defibrillator by the bathrooms. Someone grab it."

Two people rushed away from the scene. Molly continued to try and get Mr. White's heart beating again. She prayed for God's intervention in the matter. Nick knelt across from her and took his dad's hand. She saw the worry etched into the lines around his eyes, on his forehead.

"Is he going to be okay?"

"I'm going to do everything in my power to make sure he is, Nick," she said.

"Don't let him die on us, Molly." Mrs. White's face looked sickly pale. "Please."

"Here's the AED." Someone dropped the device at her feet.

Molly made eye contact with Nick. "Keep doing the chest compressions, Nick. I'm going to get the AED set up. You hear me?"

Nick nodded and took over for her as she opened the AED case and pulled out the equipment that would shock Mr. White's heart back to beating…she prayed, at least. She quickly hooked up the electrode pads to his chest. When everything was in place, she started the machine. After the first shock, she checked for Mr. White's pulse.

It was there, but faint.

"His heart is beating again," she told everyone. Relief felt palpable in the room.

"An ambulance just pulled up," someone shouted.

At that moment, EMTs rushed into the room. Molly stepped back, grateful that Mr. White had stabilized. The next few minutes were a flurry of activity as the EMTs rushed Mr. White into the ambulance. Nick and his mom went with them.

"Good work," one of the EMTs muttered to Molly. "You probably just saved this man's life."

Molly nodded, still shaken up by the whole thing. She helped save people's lives every day as a nurse, but it always felt different when the person was someone you knew.

Thank God he was okay. Thank God.

As they carried him away, Molly looked at the ground and saw the paper that had fallen out of Mr. White's hands. She reached down and picked it up. Her eyes widened at the words she saw there.

Death awaits.

FIFTEEN

It was past midnight when Nick got back to the camp. His tie was draped around the neck of his wrinkled shirt, he'd long since abandoned his sports jacket and he could feel the circles under his eyes.

What a day.

The good news was that his father was going to be okay. The doctor confirmed that he'd gone into cardiac arrest after the funeral but, thanks to Molly's quick thinking, he'd stabilized.

Nick needed to thank Molly. In the rush to get his father to the hospital, he'd forgotten. Then everything at the hospital had been a blur. Finally, his mother had sent him home to get some sleep. Thankfully, a friend from his parents' church had offered to drive him back to camp.

Molly... He shook his head at the thought of her. Would Molly even talk to him? It didn't take a professional to see that she was avoiding him this week, but the question still remained, why? He had no idea what he'd done. What had happened to make her act like this? Something with Derek, but what? The whole situation just didn't make sense to him.

He'd thought that Molly had forgiven him, that maybe they could at least be friends. He knew he couldn't ever expect more than that, because she'd never trust him again. If the woman had one thing it was self-respect.

In some ways, being in Iraq had been easier than being back here on his home turf. How ironic was that, he thought with a disgruntled chuckle.

The staff quarters were quiet when Nick slipped inside the darkened halls. Of course everyone was probably sleeping. It was late. Regardless, he tiptoed to Molly's door and looked for light coming from underneath. All was dark. Though he'd expected her to be sleeping, disappointment still weighed on him.

His thanks would have to wait until the morning. Still, the only thing he wanted at the moment was to be with Molly. He wanted to tell her how sorry he was for hurting her, how thankful he was that their paths had crossed again. How would she react when he shared his feelings?

He rubbed his face and started toward the stairs. A creak above him caught his ear. What was that sound? Was someone awake?

His steps slowed as he approached the end of the hallway. Just as he rounded the corner, someone dressed in black darted away from the stairway and toward the screen door.

"Stop!" Nick started after the man, adrenaline pulsing through him.

The man slipped outside quicker than a snake. Nick was right behind him. He reached out to grab the man, his fingers only inches away. Until the man grabbed a plastic trash can and threw it in Nick's path. Nick tumbled a moment before righting himself. It was too late. The intruder had already reached the tree line and started into the woods.

Nick didn't let up. He followed the man into the night. His dress shoes did nothing for the traction on the forest floor. The leaves underfoot made him slip, grab hold of tree branches to maintain his balance. In the meantime, the intruder inched farther away. Eventually, the man blended into the distance.

Nick stopped, his heart racing, his breathing heavy. All was quiet.

Where had the man gone? He was wearing all black, so he could disappear into the night. Was the man hiding? Or was he still running?

Nick leaned with his palms against his knees, trying to catch his breath while listening for any telltale sounds.

Nothing.

What had that been about? Had the intruder taken something from the camp? What would he have taken? The camp had nothing of value.

Nick needed to search his office and see if anything had been disturbed.

He scanned the area around him once more. All was still. With a final shake of his head, he straightened and began his walk back to the cafeteria. His legs burned on the walk and he realized that he'd come farther than he thought. His body seemed to scream for rest.

Finally, he emerged from the woods. He spotted the cafeteria ahead, lights now blazing from each window. He stepped inside and spotted Molly and Cody standing at the stairway.

Molly stepped toward him, a sweatshirt pulled on over jeans and a T-shirt. "Is everything okay? We heard yelling."

"Someone was in the cafeteria. I chased him but he got away."

Molly sucked in a breath. "In here? In this building while we slept?"

"I caught him coming down the stairs."

Molly shivered. "Creepy."

He flicked his eyes up. "Yeah, to say the least."

Cody lowered himself with a thud onto the stairs, obviously still sleepy. "What would someone want from the camp? It's not like we keep money or have anything else of value here."

"Good question. I have no idea. But we have to remember that things have been going missing around here lately. Cody, you said yourself that you felt like someone had gone through your things. And Molly, there was that missing bottle of medicine. Maybe someone from the outside did break in."

Molly sat at one of the tables. "So what now?"

"Now I'm going to go upstairs and see if I see anything missing."

"Are you going to call the sheriff?"

"Why? They won't find any evidence that someone was here. Every trail has been a dead end."

Nick blanched at his words. *Dead end.* The words had a whole new meaning to him now. He would protect this camp with his life if he had to, though.

Two hours later, Molly, Nick and Cody had searched all of the rooms upstairs to no avail. Why had someone been up there? Molly wondered. What were they searching for?

She shivered. The intruder had been in the building with her and she'd had no clue.

She pushed a box of files back into a spare closet in an upstairs office and sat on the dusty floor with a thump. She wiped some stray hairs out of her eyes with the back of her hand and leaned against the wood-paneled wall behind her. The air-conditioning hadn't been turned on in this room, and the air felt heavy with summer humidity.

Nick poked his head in the room, exhaustion showing around his eyes and in his heavy movements. "Anything?"

She shook her head. "Nothing."

He lowered himself beside her on the floor and handed her a bottle of water. "It's hot up here. Drink up."

She took the bottle and downed a long sip of water, more dehydrated than she thought. "Thanks." She turned her head toward him. They hadn't had a chance to chat since he returned to the camp, and she was anxious to talk.

"Nick, I found a note that fell from your father's hands when he had the heart attack."

"A note?"

Molly nodded. "It said 'Death awaits.'"

His face reddened. "Someone left a note for my father that said that? Is that why he had a heart attack?"

Molly shrugged and softened her voice. "Stress can cause our bodies to respond in certain ways…"

He shook his head. "I just don't get it."

"We'll need to talk to your father to see where he got the note. How's he doing, by the way?"

"He's better…thanks to you." His voice sounded soft, sincere.

"I'm glad. That was quite a scare."

"Tell me about it. My dad's always been the strong one. Seeing him like that…" Nick shook his head before letting it rest against the wall and closing his eyes. "It's enough to throw anyone off balance, you know? You never think it's going to be someone you love who's hit with something like that."

"No, you never do."

Nick turned toward her. "I really do owe you a world of thanks."

"It was nothing, Nick. I'm happy I could help." She searched his gaze a moment. "How are *you* doing?"

He shrugged. "I'm okay."

She put her hand on his knee, wanting to make sure he paid attention. "No, really. I want to hear how you're doing."

He paused a moment, his eyes flickering in thought. "I'm exhausted."

"You look tired."

He turned toward her, his eyes churning with emotions. Was he going to kiss her? Just as suddenly as the thought fluttered through Molly's mind, Nick sprang to his feet. "I need to take a walk."

"Now? At 3:00 a.m.? And with everything that's been going on around here?"

"Yeah, I just need to clear my head. Besides, I don't think whoever's behind everything will be back tonight. They've already done their dastardly deed."

She didn't want to go near the woods, especially not at this hour and after all that had happened lately. But her need to be with Nick outweighed that. "Need company?"

A bit of a spark returned to his gaze. "Are you offering?"

"Yeah, I am."

He reached for hand. "Then, yes, I need company."

Molly noticed that he didn't let go of her hand, but instead kept a firm grip on it as they went down the stairs. When they stepped outside and were embraced by the nighttime air, Molly shivered—not from the temperature, but from Nick's touch and from the events of the past few weeks. She couldn't get everything that had gone on recently out of her mind and waited tensely to hear the sound of a chainsaw in the background. But there was nothing but some crickets and gentle thunder.

They walked silently along the camp's paved loop. Molly remained quiet, sensing the need for Nick to gather his thoughts. Finally, he stopped in front of a grove of evergreen trees that lit the whole area with the fresh scent of pine. This was the place where Nick always liked to escape to gather his thoughts. He'd been like that, even as a camper.

He pulled her beneath the spindly trees and faced her, tight lines pulling at the edges of his face. "I need to tell you something, Molly."

She sucked in a breath and tried to prepare herself for whatever he had to say. Her throat felt dry as she mumbled, "Okay."

He looked to the distance a moment as if gathering his thoughts before his gaze rested on her. "I've been doing a lot of self-evaluation lately. It's part of the reason I decided to get out of the military when I had the chance. I knew I was on a path that was leading me places I didn't want go, and I was afraid if I continued on it, there would be no return."

He paused a moment, his gaze heavy and burdened. "I realized that as a chaplain I've always been there for other people. I've set my own needs aside in order to comfort others. I've set my own problems aside in order to give people a listening ear. I've set aside my opinions and feelings in order to be objective. I didn't mind doing those things. I mean, it's what I signed up for. It comes with the territory. In the process, I came to the realization that no one wanted to hear my problems or worries."

Her heart lurched as his revelation. "Nick, I—"

He squeezed her arm to shush her. "Let me finish. Please, let me get this out before I change my mind." His serious gaze locked on her. "Molly, you're one of the only people I've ever felt has really cared about me. You've listened to me and cared about me when no one else did. You've always pushed me to be real, to stop guarding my heart for long enough to let you in. I feel like you're one of the only people who can really see me… And at times I'm terrified at what that means. There are parts of me I don't want anyone to see."

"Like what?"

He shrugged. "My weaknesses. My doubt. My struggles. Living life in a fishbowl has ingrained in me that I need to be perfect."

"No one's perfect. If they were, Christ wouldn't have needed to die for us. And I'm honored that you think I can see you for who you are because I do care about you, Nick."

He shook his head. "You don't understand. You've always cared about me and, as a result, what did I do? I hurt you. I broke up with you. I let my parents speak ill of you." He paused, staring at her. A stray drop of rain splattered Molly's arm as she waited for him to finish. "I don't deserve you, Molly."

His words did something strange to Molly's heart. It welled with relief, joy, closure…wariness. "It's funny because all of these years I thought that you didn't think I was good enough for you."

He grasped the sides of her arms. "Never. Never. Do you hear me?"

Raindrops began pouring through the branches above them and hitting them like a spray of bullets. Nick grabbed her hand and pulled her several feet until they were underneath the safety of a nearby picnic shelter. The storm intensified around them. Rain battered the tin roof above them. Thunder rumbled. Lightning lit the sky.

All of Molly's senses suddenly felt alive, alert, and it had nothing to do with the storm.

She swallowed her emotions a moment. "I know you

called a friend at the hospital, Nick, to report that I was here."

Nick's eyes widened. "To report that you were here? I never did that, Molly. Where did you get that idea?"

"Derek. He said that's how he found out I was here."

"I called to do a background check and that's it." He softened his voice. "That's what all that talk about trust came from. You thought I'd turned you in? I do background checks on everyone who works here, whether paid or volunteer. It's just part of our policy."

She shook her head, suddenly feeling foolish. "I should never believe anything that Derek tells me. I don't know when I'll realize that."

Nick folded her into his arms. "I'm sorry, Molly. For everything. Everything."

"Yeah, me too." She was amazed at how safe she felt wrapped in Nick's arms with her head snugly under his chin. Few people had ever made her feel so secure and cared about. She didn't want the moment—or the feeling—to end. But doubt began to nudge its way back in. Nick had left her. Abandoned her. One moment she'd been safe and secure with him; the next he'd broken her heart. He could do it again. She could be played for the fool...again.

"Molly?"

She pulled back and looked up at him, her heart quickening again. Hope and doubt collided inside her. "Yes?"

"Do you realize where we are?"

He'd remembered. "This is the spot where we first kissed."

"Molly?"

"Yes?"

Nick's lips came down on hers, soft and sweet and full of promise. For just a moment, Molly hardly noticed the storm raging around them. Everything seemed to disappear.

He pulled away and rested his forehead against hers. "I want to give us another chance, Molly. This time, I won't screw things up."

Fear crashed through her mind. Would he leave again? Could he really be trusted with her heart? She wanted to say yes, but she still wasn't sure. And she had something to prove to herself. Running back to Nick now would only show her weakness.

She took a step back. "I can't do this. I just can't do this."

Before he could convince her otherwise, she ran back to the cafeteria.

What had just happened? Nick had thought he'd been reading the signals right. For a moment, he'd felt ready to give up his doubts and open his heart and take the plunge into a relationship. He'd thought Molly was ready, too. But maybe she'd seen something in him that he couldn't. Maybe she'd seen beyond his walls and realized she didn't like what was there.

He shook his head and took off after her. Sure, she probably needed space. But with everything going on at the camp, she also needed someone to watch her back. He'd been a fool to think they could start up again where they'd left off. He'd ruined his chances, and he had to accept that.

He walked into the staff quarters, ready to retreat to his bedroom and sulk over bad choices. He stopped in his tracks when he saw Molly standing in the hallway, her hands on her hips as she stared down the darkened corridor. "Can we talk about what just happened, Molly?"

Molly pointed in the distance, ignoring his request. "Why is Cody's door open?"

His heart still ached at her rejection, but the way she stood affirmed that something wasn't right. He had to put aside his feelings for a moment. He stepped toward the darkened room, alarms going off in his head. Cody valued his privacy and always made jokes about locking his door, even if he was only running down the hall to grab something and coming back. "That is strange. Cody?"

No answer.

He glanced at Molly, his heart even more guarded then ever. "Where would Cody be at this time of night?"

Molly shrugged. "Nowhere. He loves to sleep too much."

"Cody?"

Still no answer.

"His car is still out front," Molly said, pointing out the window.

"I have a bad feeling," Nick muttered. "I'm going to go check out his room."

Nick felt Molly step into the room behind him. Though the room looked like a typical college male's room, with an overflowing basket of laundry and a huge stash of junk food on the dresser.

She pointed to the old dresser in the corner. "Look, there's his wallet. He wouldn't have gone anywhere without it."

She was right. Cody had even bought a waterproof wallet so he could keep it with him at the pool. "I don't like this."

"Neither do I." Molly reached for a bottle atop the dresser. She read the label and suppressed a gasp. "Nick, this is one of the missing bottles of medicine."

Nick took the bottle from her and scanned the label. "Why would Cody have it?"

Molly's wide eyes focused on Nick. "Was Cody the one who stole the medicine? That just doesn't seem like Cody."

"But if he didn't steal them, how did they end up on his dresser?"

Molly held the bottle up to the light. "The pills are missing from inside it." She shook the bottle. "It looks like a piece of paper is in this one."

"Let's open it and see what it is."

With shaky fingers, she pulled the paper out, unfolded it and smoothed the crinkles. Nick stood behind her, anxious to see what the paper said. The words came into focus.

Shut down the camp or Cody will die.

SIXTEEN

The next morning, a crowd gathered at the camp to do an extensive search of the camp's land. If Cody was here, they would find him. They had to. Nick wouldn't be able to live with himself if they didn't.

Nick saw the sheriff in the distance, talking to a group of people, and approached him, ready to find out their next move. Sheriff Spruill cut his conversation short and pulled Nick aside. "Nick, we did a flyover this morning in one of the crop dusters. I thought you would want to know that there are two other places on the camp's property where there are trees missing."

"Two other places? What sense does that make?"

"A friend with the forestry extension office also paid a visit to the camp this morning. He checked out that first batch of trees that had been cut down. I think I know what's going on here."

"What's that? Don't keep me in suspense." Molly approached them, turning Nick's thoughts momentarily away from the conversation as her fruity scent drifted toward him.

The sheriff rubbed his chin. "The trees that were cut down are black walnuts that were probably eighty years old."

"Okay, that makes sense. My granddad loved trees. He probably planted them there himself when he was a boy. It wouldn't surprise me."

"Well, you've got groves and groves of them on your property. You have any idea what those trees would earn someone on the black market?"

Nick shrugged. "I don't know. A few thousands dollars."

"Five of them would give someone a paycheck of somewhere around a hundred thousand dollars."

"A hundred grand? You've got to be kidding me."

"Black walnut is sought after in the furniture business." The sheriff looked at Molly. "Which brings us to the man you ran over on your way to the camp. He was a furniture maker from Germany and had apparently come to town to do some business. The only thing we don't know is who's selling these trees."

Molly nodded slowly as if processing everything. "So someone discovered them on the camp's property and realized they could make a fortune. How many stumps did you find?"

"Fifteen."

Nick's eyebrows shot up. "That's no small chunk of change."

"No, it's not."

Nick's gaze traveled to the woods in the distance. "So now we just have to figure out who's behind the tree theft. Is this common? I never even stopped to think that maybe someone was cutting down my trees in order to sell them."

"I wouldn't call it common, but it does happen. My gut tells me that Gene probably discovered what was happening and that's why someone ended his life. Whoever's doing this isn't playing games. We're checking with the state police to see if they pulled over any logging trucks within the past month or so. Whoever is doing this is only steps away from being caught."

"We can only hope. Any word on Cody?"

The sheriff shook his head. "We're out there combing the woods now, but so far we haven't heard anything. His mom is worried sick. Rightfully so."

A worried wrinkle formed between Molly's eyebrows. "What can we do to help?"

Before the sheriff answered, two men from the search party came running from the woods. "Sheriff, we found something."

"Well, what is it?"

The tall, lanky man gasped for breath. "We think you need to see it yourself. Nick and Molly, too."

Nick and Molly exchanged a glance. The group took off into the woods. More than anything, Nick wanted to put his hand at Molly's elbow, to help guide her through this wilderness. But she'd made it clear they had no future together. He had to accept that. Despite that realization, his gaze constantly went to her, soaking in her beauty.

He should have never let her slip through his fingers. Never.

But right now they had other things to worry about.

They stopped at the remnants of a small campfire in the forest. Nick shook his head. What was so important about this site that he and Molly had to come?

One of the volunteers pointed to the edge of the fire. Nick took a step closer and squinted. There, in the ashes, were pictures of Nick and Molly taken throughout the last couple of weeks. One of them talking at the field of fire-flies. Another of them sitting by the campfire. One of them laughing together, both looking content, happy. His gaze moved beyond the gut-clenching pictures, and he saw the Chainsaw Charlie doll that had scared Molly on her first night of camp and a white baseball cap with the name of a pharmaceutical company across it. The white material was stained with blood.

The sheriff squatted down beside it, using a nearby stick to raise the singed hat into the air. "This isn't Cody's, is it?"

Nick shook his head, trying to remember if he'd ever seen it before. "I don't think so."

Molly cleared her throat. "No, it's mine. Someone must have gotten it from my quarters."

Nick didn't like this. He didn't like this one bit.

The sheriff pulled his lips into a tight line. "I'd say they're trying to send you a message."

Molly nodded. "I'd say it's working."

Enough was enough. Nick wanted to keep the camp open, but Cody's life wasn't worth it. He'd had some crazy dreams about reviving the camp and making it back into the place it had once been. That wouldn't be happening, though. There were too many obstacles. All of this had been a whim, an opportunity that dropped unexpectedly into his lap. Now it was clear that the camp had gone too far downhill to fix—just like the possibility of a relationship with Molly. He needed to get on with his life. He'd been feeling sorry for himself for too long. He should just take the job at his dad's church and accept his choices for what they were.

Nick drew himself up straight, resolve hardening his muscles. "That settles it."

Sheriff Spruill stood. "Settles what?"

"I'm shutting the camp down. For good."

Molly stepped toward, her eyes wide with alarm and surprise. "Why would you do that?"

"There comes a point where you have to see the writing

on the wall. I'm going to accept the position at my dad's church and go on with life just as I'm expected to do."

"Nick…"

His scowl greeted her. "Enough is enough, Molly. I'm done."

And with that, he stomped back toward the camp.

Molly lay in bed that evening, staring at the ceiling above and praying for sleep to find her.

Cody still hadn't been found. The search had come up with nothing except Molly's bloody baseball cap. Thankfully, the blood had been tested and it wasn't human. Still, Molly prayed that Cody was okay and that he'd be found soon.

Nick's words replayed in her head. Would Nick really shut down the camp? She could understand his frustration to an extent. All of this would pass eventually. But at what cost, she wondered.

Nick had told her earlier that she could stay another week. That would give her time to find something new, he'd insisted. But then she needed to be gone.

She could tell he was hurt by her rejection. But she and Nick could never be together again. She would only be setting herself up for more heartbreak, especially now that he was taking the position at his father's church. She had to prove to herself that she was not her mom. She could stand on her own two feet. She was worthy of respect.

So why did her heart hurt so much?

A sound outside her door caught her ear. Was that the squeaky screen door opening? Had Nick gone somewhere? She climbed on her knees and peered out the window blinds above her bed. The woods stared back at her.

Perhaps Molly had been hearing things.

Still, she sat on the edge of the bed, perched for fight or flight. Several minutes of silence passed.

She'd simply been hearing things, she concluded. She pulled her legs back under the covers.

Then she heard a creak in the hallway. That was definitely a creak. And it was close. Someone was outside her room, she realized.

Her breathing intensified. She needed a plan and fast. Her gaze skimmed her surroundings. Nothing she could use as a weapon.

She watched the door handle and saw it slowly turn.

She blinked, trying to convince herself that she was imagining things.

But she knew she wasn't. Someone was trying to get into her room.

Quickly—quietly—she darted behind the door. Best-case scenario, she could take the intruder by surprise and then flee from the room. Worst-case scenario... Well, she didn't want to go there.

Suddenly, the knob released. A swish came from beneath the door. Molly's gaze rushed to the crack under the door where she saw a white piece of paper. Holding her breath, she reached for the paper. Her hands trembled as she fumbled to open the folds.

Even in the dark, she could read the crudely written words.

Nick's next.

Her heart pounded in her ears. She had to talk to him. Now.

She hesitated with her hand on the door for only a moment. Sure, the intruder could still be out there. But she had to get upstairs. She had to warn Nick.

Her sweaty hands slid across the metal before finally

finding traction. Everything looked peaceful on the other side, no evidence that anyone had been here.

She scrambled upstairs. Her hip knocked into a table with a rotary phone on it on the way and a device crashed to the floor with a jangle. If the intruder was still in the building, her location was no secret now.

She raised her hand to pound on Nick's door when she noticed it wasn't latched. With bated breath, she pushed it open. An empty bed waited on the other side.

She closed her eyes a moment. Where was he? The office?

She scrambled down the hallway, but found the office empty also. Where was he? Had the intruder already gotten to him?

Hurrying back down the stairs, she decided to try his cell phone. It often didn't work out here, but she'd try anyway. Just as she put the phone back on the receiver, the device jangled. She froze a moment, expecting the worst, before answering.

"Molly?"

She recognized the voice immediately—Nick's mom. She didn't have time for this.

"Mrs. White, Nick's in danger. You've got to call the sheriff for me and tell him to come out to the camp."

"In danger? What do you mean?"

"I don't have time to explain. Please. Just do it. I'm going to go see if I can find him."

Before Mrs. White could argue, Molly hung up and dialed Nick's cell phone. It went straight to voice mail. Where was he?

The grove, she realized. That's where he always went when he wanted to think. Was that where he was now? She had to check.

She ran down the path toward the grove, ignoring the

woods lurking nearby. *Think about Nick,* she chanted silently. She had to find him. The tree thieves couldn't have found him yet.

Finally, she reached the grove. Her gaze scanned the area. Empty. No one was there.

She leaned over and tried to catch her breath. The first tear popped to her eyes. *Nick. Where are you? I thought for sure you'd be here. What if...?*

She couldn't let her thoughts go there. Maybe he was somewhere else. But where?

Movement clattered behind her. She straightened, realizing how foolish she'd been to come out here alone. She should have waited for the sheriff, but she'd been so desperate to find Nick. Her need to warn him had outweighed her safety. She twirled around.

"Molly?"

"Nick?" He jumped down from his perch in a live oak, brushing the dirt from his jeans and looking at her, perplexed. She raced to him and threw her arms around him. "What were you doing?"

His expression remained pinched, concerned. "Thinking. Praying. What are you doing here?"

She grasped his arm as the ominous threat slammed back into her mind. "Nick, we've got to get out of here. Someone broke into the staff quarters and left me a note saying that you're next."

His eyebrows drew together. "I'm next?"

She nodded quickly, urgently as she grasped his hand and tugged him. "We need to get out of here. Now."

He took a step away. "Okay. Let's go."

They'd only taken a few steps when a deep voice beckoned behind them. "Why couldn't you two just take the hint and leave?"

Molly and Nick froze. She was too late. The person

behind Gene's murder and Cody's kidnapping had found them. Now they would be just two more casualties of this crime spree.

Slowly, they both turned around. A man in a black mask emerged from the woods, a gun pointed straight at them. Though Molly could only see his eyes, she saw the evil in their depths.

SEVENTEEN

Nick stared at the gun and swiftly moved Molly behind him. The seriousness of the situation pressed on him. Life or death. He was going to fight to ensure life won over death—Molly's life in particular. "What do you want with us?"

"I want you to come with me."

Nick shook his head, determined to keep his voice even. "We're not going anywhere with you. Why don't you put that gun down so we can talk?"

"Nothing to talk about." The man raised his gun and fired a shot. Molly screamed and clutched him tighter. "Next shot goes into the girl. Now move."

Nick raised his hands. "No need for anyone to get hurt. Why don't you just let me go with you? Leave Molly out of this."

"No. Both of you. Into the woods. Now." He pointed with his gun toward the forest.

"But—"

The man pistol-whipped Nick across the temple. Pain screamed across his head, and his hands went to his hairline. He could feel the blood there.

"Nick!" Molly reached for him.

"I'm okay, Molly."

"One more word and a bullet goes through the girl. Need I say more?"

Nick reached for Molly's hand, grimacing. "We're coming."

Nick saw the fear on Molly's face, in her wide eyes and pale skin. He had to protect her, had to keep her safe. But how would he do that when a gun-wielding maniac was merely feet away?

Lord, help us.

They stepped into the woods, the man right behind them. Nick kept a tight grip on Molly's hand as they plunged into the dark wilderness. The foliage was thick here and the low branches that didn't block their way grabbed at them, snaring their skin and clothes. Molly's hand trembled in his.

"Keep moving." The man shoved his gun into Nick's back.

"You can have the trees, you know. Nothing's worth a life."

The man grunted.

They had to split up, Nick realized. The man couldn't chase both of them. It might give Molly a chance to get away before the man harmed her—or worst.

"Keep going straight until you reach the creek," the man ordered.

Why did his voice sound familiar? Nick had a feeling he knew the man; he just couldn't place the voice. The man seemed to keep his speech low, as if on purpose.

Nick kept hold of Molly's hand and began tapping out a message on her palm, just like they'd done as teenagers. Only when they were teenagers, they'd tapped out sweet messages of love and romance. Right now, Nick tapped out "go left." He prayed that she got the message. When he finished, he glanced over at her. She gave a subtle nod. Good, she understood.

Their feet slipped atop the underbrush and rocks leading to the creek bed. Nick's heart began beating double-time as scenarios on how his plan would play out began racing through his mind.

He'd distract the gunman while Molly got away. She could follow the creek until she reached his grandfather's cabin. From there, hopefully she could find her way back to the camp. He prayed she could.

They reached the creek. It was now or never. Nick squeezed Molly's hand. As she let go, Nick swung toward the man behind him.

Molly glanced back and saw Nick wrestle the gunman to the ground. She started to reach out, desperate to help. But how?

"Go!" Nick yelled.

She had to run. Nick was risking his life so that she might have a chance. She couldn't let the opportunity be wasted.

"Now!" Nick shouted.

"Get her!" Another man appeared out of nowhere and started toward Molly.

She darted into the woods. She couldn't stay near the creek—certainly it would be too easy to find her if she did. So instead she used the woods as a cover. She crept between the trees and around rocks and stumps, hoping to conceal herself.

The deeper into the woods she got, the faster her heart raced. Sweat covered her palms and forehead. Shakes started from deep inside and traveled until they reached the tips of her fingers.

Was Nick okay? What if the masked man had shot him?

Tears pushed to her eyes again. She couldn't think like that. She had to think about staying hidden, about getting back to the camp so she could tell the sheriff what was going on.

A twig snapped in the distance. The second gunman was still on her trail. She had to keep moving, keep going forward.

Her feet slipped at an embankment and she began sliding downward, toward the creek. She couldn't hit the creek. If she did, there was no way she'd gain her footing enough to escape from the madman chasing her.

Finally, she caught a root that jutted out. Her body jerked to a halt.

The dark water waited to swallow her up below. If her hand slipped, she'd be submerged into the swamplike water beneath her. But a madman waited above her. What was she going to do?

Another footfall sounded. Her pursuer was gaining ground. She couldn't stay here, in plain sight.

Taking a deep breath, she released the root and slid the rest of the way down the hill. Her body hit the murky water, its coolness sending a shock through her. She put aside her thoughts of snakes and other gruesome creatures that lived there. Instead, she pushed to the surface and clawed at the mud on the other side.

She looked back for long enough to see a man standing at the top of the hill, his gun pointed at her.

Nick grasped the gunman's shoulders and slammed him into the ground. The man's hand hit a rock, and the gun scattered to the ground.

At least the fight was fair now. Man against man.

He only prayed that the man's accomplice hadn't reached Molly yet.

His attacker drew back and charged at him. They rolled down the hill toward the creek. Stumps and roots and briars assaulted them. Nick didn't care. He knew there were more important things. He knew he was fighting for his life.

Finally, they rammed into an oak tree. Both stopped with a jolt. Nick's attacker moaned—but only for a moment. Just as quickly, he pulled his hand back and jammed his fist toward Nick.

Nick rolled out of the way and the man's fist slammed into the ground. He grunted, a maniacal persistence about him.

Molly. How was Molly?

If Nick was going to find out, he had to defeat this man first.

Nick pulled in a last burst of adrenaline. He charged toward the masked man until his attacker sprawled backward on the ground. His head hit a rock and man laid motionless.

Unconscious.

Nick crept forward, watching for any sign of movement. Nothing except the steady rise and fall of the man's chest. Carefully, he leaned down and jerked the man's mask off. He blinked at the face that had once been concealed.

"Ricky Balderston?" he muttered. Ernie's son. Was Ernie in on this also?

Nick had to find Molly. Now.

Molly stared at the gun. Would the man actually use it?

As if he'd read her mind, wood splintered on the tree beside her. The man was shooting at her, and she stayed in one place like a sitting duck. Quickly, she turned on her heel and took off. Deeper and deeper into the woods she ran. Bullets flew around her, and she thanked God the man wasn't a good shot.

Finally she stopped running and took a moment to catch her breath. She paused, listening for the telltale signs of someone around her. Nothing. Could she have lost him?

Her body ached. Her wet clothes clung to her. And the nighttime chill began to seep into her bones.

Her gaze flickered around her. Trees, trees and more trees.

Where was she?

She knew—she was in the woods. Lost.

Her shakes intensified.

The darkness surrounded her. The trees reached for her. And suddenly she felt like a little girl again. She sat down against a tree and pulled her knees to her chest.

How would she get away from the killer? And even if she did manage that, how would she get back to the camp? Which way had she come from, even? Now that she'd stopped, everything looked the same, every direction seemed familiar yet unfamiliar. How long would it take someone to find her on these four hundred acres? Would a wild animal get to her first? The gunman?

Her shivers couldn't be controlled. Her teeth began chattering. Imaginary spiders crept up her skin. The trees began to creak. A shadow passed overhead. An intruder? No, she was the intruder here.

She leaned back into the tree as despair bit deep.

The woods had taken her captive again.

Nick wanted to call for Molly, but he couldn't make himself known with a gunman on the loose. Instead, he followed the creek, hoping to see a sign of the woman he hoped to spend the rest of his life with.

Would he have a chance to tell her that?

He prayed he would.

All of these years he felt like he'd been following a path he hadn't wanted to take. God had used him there and he'd grown as a person. But now he was ready to follow God on this new path, on this second chance. A second chance that included Molly, he hoped. Faced with death right now, his faith became clear to him. His faith was his own—not simply something his parents had pushed on him. He knew without a doubt that God existed and that He had a plan for their lives, despite all of the ups and downs.

Please don't let things end poorly, Lord. I want to follow where You lead. I'll go wherever You want me to go. But protect Molly.

Something red in the distance caught his attention. Quietly, he approached the object, careful not to be heard. He reached a jagged tree limb and pulled a piece of cloth from a protruding branch. Molly's sweatshirt. Part of it had been torn off. He glanced below at the swamp water. Had she slipped down this embankment into the water? Was she on the other side now? It was his best lead so far—his only lead, for that matter.

He wandered alongside the creek for a moment until he found a tree that had fallen over the water. Carefully, he maneuvered across. When Nick had thought she'd stayed on the other side of the creek, his search perimeter was narrower. But now a whole new search area waited.

How would he find her?

Would the gunman find her first?

He followed the creek farther until he reached a part where the banks looked disturbed and muddy. Could this be where Molly got out? It was the best lead he had yet. Following his gut, he climbed the bank, his feet sinking into the mud, and headed deeper into the woods.

Molly hated the woods, and this area was so thick with

trees. If someone didn't know what they were doing, they could easily get turned around. And, though not common, there had been black bears and wildcats spotted on occasion in this area.

He paused for a moment beside an elm tree and listened. A twig snapped in the distance.

Ernie?

Slowly, he peered around the tree. Sure enough, he spotted Ernie mere feet away creeping through the woods, gun in his hand.

The man's gaze and each movement looked purposeful. He was on the prowl, searching for Molly. Anger surged through Nick at the thought. He had to take Ernie down.

He stalked him. Then, on the count of three, he lunged at the man.

Just as he tackled him to the ground, the gun blasted.

Molly's teeth chattered still and a spiderweb had somehow draped itself over her face. As much as she wiped her eyes, strands of the web still clung to her.

She had to get a grip. She could get out of this.

She prayed for clear thinking. Panicking would do her no good.

She knew from watching the sunrise at the flagpole every morning that the area on this side of the creek was to the west of the camp. When the sun began rising in the morning, she would follow the light, and hopefully it would lead her to the creek and then to the camp. Right now, she decided to stay put. Wandering around in the woods might only serve to get her deeper into the forest. She had to stay calm.

Was Nick okay? The only thing that seemed to settle her nerves was when she thought about something other than her own predicament. What had happened back there where she'd left him? Was the sheriff here yet? Had he found Nick?

What if Nick hadn't made it?

What if no one came to look for her? Just like when she was a child. Her mom hadn't even noticed she was gone until the evening. By that time, Molly had been deep into the woods. It was a miracle she'd even been found.

She closed her eyes. But she'd been found. That was what she had to hold on to. She'd been found.

The sound of gunfire pulled her out of one fear and into another.

The gun blast had been close. Close enough that her ears rang for a moment at the loudness.

She couldn't stay here. She had to move. What if that was Nick who'd just been shot? What if he needed her help?

She stood, shivers still racking her entire body. All around her stood darkness as black as she'd ever seen.

Staying low, she crept along beside the underbrush, trying to keep herself concealed. Her fear and the cold temperatures kept her shivering. She pressed forward, ignoring the briars that grabbed at her ankles.

Shouting echoed in the distance. Who was that? Nick? And who else?

Another gunshot cracked the air. She lifted up a prayer. *Please let Nick be okay.*

Clarity hit her at once.

Nick was nothing like the men her mom had dated. She had to forgive him for breaking her heart, and she had to forgive herself for the bad relationship she'd had with Derek. But Nick wasn't Derek. Nick was a good man, one who'd be willing to give up his life for her. He'd proven that time and time again.

Now was the time to get past her fears—both about

relationships and the maniac chasing her through the woods. She had to be willing to take a chance again or she'd risk dying a worst kind of death—the death of hope.

She stopped behind a thick tree. Slowly, she peered around. Mere feet away she saw Nick wrestling with... Ernie? He was the one behind this? No wonder he'd tried to paint Cody in a negative light when she'd first met him. He'd been trying to take any suspicion off himself.

Her throat felt dry as she contemplated her next move. She had to help before the gun went off again and a bullet pierced Nick.

She glanced around and spotted a rock. She crawled over the moist, prickly terrain until she reached it. Carefully, she lifted it from the dirt and crept back toward Nick. Crouching low, she waited for the right moment.

Nick jerked Ernie onto his back. Ernie's hand flopped to the side. The gun still remained in his hand. Just as Nick pinned one of Ernie's hands, the man raised his gun toward Nick.

Molly let out a yell as she burst from behind the tree. Before Ernie could realize what was happening, she slammed the rock onto his hand. The gun scattered across the forest floor as Ernie scrunched his face in pain. Quickly, Molly grabbed it and pointed it at the groundskeeper.

"Don't make any moves," she yelled, wiping some dirt from her cheek and gasping in a deep breath.

Nick took the gun from her wobbly hold, his eyes assessing her. "You're okay?"

Molly nodded, wanting to fall into his arms and tell him just how much she cared about him. Before she could, Ernie grunted, grasping his hand.

"Why couldn't you two just have let it go? No one else had to get hurt."

Nick kept the gun aimed at him. "Why? Why would you do this?"

Ernie grunted again. "I got debts to pay. Mowing the grass at the camp wasn't cutting it. I needed a lot of money and fast. When I saw those trees, I knew I'd hit the jackpot."

Molly shook her head in disbelief. "Debts? What kind of debt do you have?"

He shrugged. "Gambling. The money problems were about to ruin my marriage."

A twig snapped in the distance and a flashlight bobbed toward them.

"Identify yourself," Nick ordered.

"It's me, Sheriff Spruill." The sheriff's face came into view, and he looked down at the man on the ground, shaking his head. "Ernie Balderston, you're under arrest." The sheriff looked up at them. "I've got it from here. Paramedics are waiting at the camp to look you two over. Can you find your way back there?"

Nick nodded. "I can get us there." He turned to Molly. "You're okay to walk?"

"Yeah, I can do that."

As the sheriff began leading Ernie away in handcuffs, Nick turned toward her. "I was so worried." He pressed his lips into her forehead.

"All I could think about was that you'd been shot, Nick. I couldn't stand the thought of it."

"God brought us both through this."

Molly looked up at him, her heart warm and sure. "For a reason."

A smile stretched across Nick's face. "For a reason." He slipped an arm around her shoulders. "Come on. We've got to get you back before you get hypothermia."

* * *

Molly refused to stay in the hospital bed. Instead, she lowered herself onto one of the padded chairs at the bedside. There was really no need for her to be admitted. All she'd needed was a warm shower, some blankets and some coffee and she would have been fine. But Nick had insisted that she be checked out.

As she pulled a blanket around her, she looked up and saw three people standing in the doorway. Her eyes widened. "Please. Come in."

Nick and his parents stepped inside the cramped hospital room.

Nick's dad smiled down at her. "Just as they're letting me go home, you got admitted. How's that for luck?"

"I won't be here long. In fact, they're probably going to let me go home sometime today."

Nick kissed her cheek. "Is that what you said or what the doctor said? I'm pretty sure that nurses make the worst patients."

"I'm pretty sure you're right." Her smile slipped when she looked up at Mrs. White. She cleared her throat. "Thanks for coming."

"There's something I need to say to you, Molly." Mrs. White wrung her hands together a moment, whatever she had to say obviously weighing heavy on her mind. "I was wrong. I don't say that very often, but apparently I ought to." She let out a small laugh. "No one likes to be around self-righteous people. I know that.

"I'm sorry, Molly, for the way I've treated you. You didn't deserve it. I guess the truth is that I don't feel like anyone is good enough for my boy. If you ever have kids, you'll understand. But that's neither here nor there. I came to apologize. I saw that you were willing to risk your life for my son, and I knew that if Nicholas had someone who loved him that much that he was a lucky man."

"You mean that?"

She nodded. "I do. I'm sorry, and I'm trying to change. It wasn't until I thought I might have lost Nicholas that I realized how pious I've been acting. Do you forgive me?"

"Of course."

Mrs. White squeezed her hand. "Thank you, Molly." She straightened. "Now I'll give you two some time together. Good to see you, dear."

"You, too."

When they disappeared out of the room, Molly turned to Nick. "I never thought I'd have that conversation."

"Me neither. I'm glad you did, though. I'm really glad."

"Did they find Cody?"

"They did. Ernie had rented a garage out in the country. It's where he was running all of his illegal tree-theft operations. Cody was tied up there. But he's okay. Nothing a few hamburgers and some time with friends won't fix. Ernie had been blackmailing Cody, saying he would tell everyone he was dating a camper, which is strictly against the rules."

"Was he?"

Nick shook his head. "Cody says no, that they were just friends. Ernie was trying to set Cody up by planting the medicine in his room. But Cody figured out what was going on and that's when Ernie decided to use him as a pawn in his twisted little game."

"Ernie was really behind all of this. That just seems crazy."

"He was. He claims he didn't mean to kill Gene. Gene walked into the woods one day and found them while they were cutting the trees. They got into a fistfight and Gene fell onto one of the trees. The head injury killed him. Ernie stashed his body in the cabin hoping it would look like a wild animal got him."

"And how about the man I hit on my way here? Why did Ernie kill him?"

"The man began to suspect that something wasn't legal. He threatened to tell the authorities. Ernie knew he couldn't let that happen. Apparently, he'd accumulated hundreds of thousands of dollars in debt. He killed the man, and then tried to find a new buyer for the wood. In the meantime, he found your employment application and placed it in the man's coat, trying to take any suspicion off himself by sending the sheriff on a wild-goose chase."

"That's so awful," Molly said, then paused. "I talked to one of my friends in Maryland this morning. We worked at the hospital together."

"Are you going back to your old job?"

She chuckled at his worried expression. "No, but she did tell me that Dr. Derek Houston is under investigation. Apparently, he tried to frame another nurse on staff there. She recorded everything from the start, so she has evidence that he was trying to manipulate the situation."

"Good. He deserves some justice." He leaned toward her. "There is some good news to this whole crazy situation."

"And what's that?"

"I realized that I could sell the trees on the land and make enough money to not only keep the camp afloat but also to do some upgrades."

"That's great news, Nick. So you're going to be sticking around?"

He nodded. "I am. You know how we both wanted to be missionaries when we were teens? I think this camp is my mission field. It will give me the chance to work in my area of gifting. I can use my hands and be outdoors, but still work with people."

Molly grinned. "I think you'll be great."

"God's really been teaching me a lot lately, Molly. I can't live with all of these walls up around my heart. Really, it's an isolated existence and life isn't meant to be lived alone. I've realized that I'm going to make mistakes and I'm going to disappoint people, but that's just a part of life. You helped me to realize that, Molly. You've always accepted me—warts, and all. Thank you."

She squeezed his hand. "I'm happy for you. I've had a few realizations of my own. I've had this crazy fear of making stupid mistakes and turning out the same way my mother did. It's why I wanted to keep you at a distance. To run back into the arms of someone who I thought had abandoned me would make me seem weak. But I've realized that you didn't really abandon me, Nick. We both needed time to grow up and figure out who we were. God brought us back together at the perfect time. His timing is always right."

"His timing is perfect." Nick's expression turned serious. "I know you think that your relationship with the doctor made you seem weak, but I really think it showed your strength, Molly."

"How so?"

"Because if you were weak, you would have stayed with him. Instead, you stood up to him. You remained firm against his charm. That shows strength."

"Maybe you're right."

"I think I am." He smiled. "Well, you asked me this, so how about you? You're going to stick around, aren't you?"

"If there's a place for me."

"Oh, there's a place for you." He got down on one knee. "I realized last night that I never wanted to lose you again.

Molly Hamilton, I want to marry you. I want you to be my wife. And together, I want us to work at Camp Hope Springs."

Molly threw her arms around him. "Nothing would make me happier. I love you, Nick White."

"I love you, Molly Hamilton."

EPILOGUE

Molly adjusted the wildflower bouquet in her hands one more time before stepping from the nurse's quarters into the cafeteria. It was amazing how the room had been transformed into something casually elegant. White tablecloths draped the tables; flowers and ribbons decorated their tops. Gauze hung in swags over the windows.

This was really happening, Molly realized.

Laura stuck her head into the cafeteria and grinned when she spotted Molly. "It's time."

Molly brushed some microscopic lint from her white sundress and stepped outside into the glorious late-summer afternoon. In the distance, she heard a guitar plucking out a familiar melody. Slowly, she made her way down a little hill toward the vespers area at Camp Hope Springs.

This was the very place at the camp where Molly had dedicated her life to serving God ten years ago. How appropriate that today she would be getting married here and beginning a new journey here at Camp Hope Springs.

Just a few weeks ago, this camp had been practically falling apart. But with the money the camp had received from the black walnut trees, they'd redone the entire area. Now it looked like something from a fairy tale.

Various people who'd attended camp this summer sat on the wooden, hillside benches. She passed Cody, the sheriff and several board members from the camp. She hardly saw them. Instead, she saw Nick standing at the end of the path wearing khakis and a white button-down shirt. He'd never looked so handsome.

Beside him stood his father, the Bible open in his hands as he readied himself to perform the marriage ceremony.

Molly reached the end and took Nick's hands into her own. He leaned toward her. "You look beautiful."

"Thank you."

She glanced at the front bench where Mrs. White sat. The woman flashed a grin toward Molly. Thank goodness their differences had finally been mended. Now Nick and Molly could move forward with his parents' blessings. Another answered prayer.

As his dad began the ceremony, Molly felt the familiar tap on her palm.

I love you.

Molly smiled. She interrupted the ceremony as she leaned forward and gave Nick a quick kiss. The audience burst into laughter, as did Nick's father.

"I don't say this very often, but this time I truly believe it," Mr. White said. "You two are a match made in heaven and I know you're going to do great things here at this camp. And without further ado, I now pronounce you husband and wife. You may kiss the bride…or the groom…or each other. Again."

Chuckles filled the air around them. Nick and Molly sealed their marriage with a kiss and began their sweet new life at Camp Hope Springs.

Nick's grandfather had been right. Hope could spring from even the direst of circumstances. All one had to have was a little faith.

* * * * *

Dear Reader,

I grew up going to Christian summer camp and have so many good memories of my time there. After high school, I traveled, representing my college on a music and drama team for two summers and ended up back at Christian summer camps throughout the Midwest. Camp can be such a life-changing place. But I still do remember some of those campfire stories. Before I started writing this book, I started asking myself the golden question of "what if…." That's when this book was born. I hope you enjoyed *Ricochet* and remember that, with God on our side, we truly can bounce back from hard circumstances and come out stronger than before.

Christy Barritt

Questions for Discussion

1. Did you ever go to summer camp? What are some of your favorite memories of your time there?

2. Where's a place that positive life change happened for you—if not at camp, then maybe a retreat or church service or mission trip? What brought about that life change?

3. In *Ricochet,* Nick's parents have discounted Molly without even getting to know her. Has anyone ever judged you like this? How did it make you feel?

4. Have you ever discounted someone without getting to know them? Why?

5. How can we push past other people's perceptions of us and become the person God's created us to be? What holds you back from being who you were created to be?

6. Molly gives up her career and flees to Camp Hope Springs after a false accusation is made against her. Has anyone ever said anything about you that isn't true? How did you handle it?

7. Nick feels like he's spent his life in a fishbowl—a place where everyone is constantly watching him. It comes to the point where he doesn't know if his faith is real or if he's just going through the motions. Can you relate? How do you keep your relationship with God fresh and real?

8. Nick has also made a lot of life choices based on his parents' expectations of him. Have you ever made a choice based on others' expectations? How did it work out?

9. Are there any unfair expectations that you've put on others around you? Is this something you need to change?

10. Are there any life circumstances that you need to bounce back from? What are they? What's the first step in moving past them?

REQUEST YOUR FREE BOOKS!

2 FREE RIVETING INSPIRATIONAL NOVELS
PLUS 2 FREE MYSTERY GIFTS

Love Inspired.
SUSPENSE

YES! Please send me 2 FREE Love Inspired® Suspense novels and my 2 FREE mystery gifts (gifts are worth about $10). After receiving them, if I don't wish to receive any more books, I can return the shipping statement marked "cancel". If I don't cancel, I will receive 4 brand-new novels every month and be billed just $4.49 per book in the U.S. or $4.99 per book in Canada. That's a saving of at least 22% off the cover price. It's quite a bargain! Shipping and handling is just 50¢ per book in the U.S. and 75¢ per book in Canada.* I understand that accepting the 2 free books and gifts places me under no obligation to buy anything. I can always return a shipment and cancel at any time. Even if I never buy another book, the two free books and gifts are mine to keep forever.

123/323 IDN FEHR

Name	(PLEASE PRINT)	

Address		Apt. #

City	State/Prov.	Zip/Postal Code

Signature (if under 18, a parent or guardian must sign)

Mail to the **Reader Service:**
IN U.S.A.: P.O. Box 1867, Buffalo, NY 14240-1867
IN CANADA: P.O. Box 609, Fort Erie, Ontario L2A 5X3

Not valid for current subscribers to Love Inspired Suspense books.

**Are you a subscriber to Love Inspired Suspense
and want to receive the larger-print edition?
Call 1-800-873-8635 or visit www.ReaderService.com.**

* Terms and prices subject to change without notice. Prices do not include applicable taxes. Sales tax applicable in N.Y. Canadian residents will be charged applicable taxes. Offer not valid in Quebec. This offer is limited to one order per household. All orders subject to credit approval. Credit or debit balances in a customer's account(s) may be offset by any other outstanding balance owed by or to the customer. Please allow 4 to 6 weeks for delivery. Offer available while quantities last.

Your Privacy—The Reader Service is committed to protecting your privacy. Our Privacy Policy is available online at www.ReaderService.com or upon request from the Reader Service.

We make a portion of our mailing list available to reputable third parties that offer products we believe may interest you. If you prefer that we not exchange your name with third parties, or if you wish to clarify or modify your communication preferences, please visit us at www.ReaderService.com/consumerschoice or write to us at Reader Service Preference Service, P.O. Box 9062, Buffalo, NY 14269. Include your complete name and address.

When Greta Goodloe is jilted by her longtime sweetheart, she takes comfort in matchmaking between newcomer Luke Starns and her schoolmarm sister. Yet the more Greta tries to throw them together, the more Luke fascinates her.

Read on for a sneak peek of A GROOM FOR GRETA by Anna Schmidt, available October 2012 from Love Inspired® Historical.

***

"So what do you intend to do about this turn of events, Luke?"

"Do? Your sister made her feelings plain last evening. She does not wish to spend her time with me."

Greta sighed heavily. "She does not know what she wants. The question is, are you serious about finding a wife for yourself or not?"

"I am quite serious."

"Then—"

"What I will not do," Luke interrupted, "is go after a woman who has declared openly that she has no interest in making a home with me."

"And what of her idea that you and I should…" She let the sentence trail off.

"That depends," he said slowly.

"On what?"

"On whether or not you are able to put aside your feelings for Josef Bontrager. Your sister believes that your feelings for him were not as strong as they should be for two people planning a life together. Do you agree?"

"Lydia is…I mean…oh, I don't know," Greta replied.

"How can either of you expect me to know what it is that I'm feeling these days? It's too soon."

"If Josef came to you and asked for your forgiveness and pleaded with you to reconsider, would you?"

"No," she finally whispered. "I would not."

Luke felt his heart pounding, and he realized that over the months he had been in Celery Fields, he had taken more notice of the beautiful Greta Goodloe than he had allowed himself to admit. He had learned a hard lesson back in Ontario and he had been determined not to make the same mistake twice.

But if Greta had come to realize that Josef was not for her…

On the other hand, surely the idea that she might be firm in her decision to be rid of Josef did not mean that she was ready for someone new.

***

*Don't miss A GROOM FOR GRETA by Anna Schmidt,
the next heartwarming book
in the AMISH BRIDES OF CELERY FIELDS series,
on sale October 2012 wherever Love Inspired® Historical
books are sold!*

Love Inspired

⟵ TEXAS TWINS ⟶

Follow the adventure of two sets of twins who are torn
apart by family secrets and learn to find their way home.

Her Surprise Sister by Marta Perry
July 2012

Mirror Image Bride by Barbara McMahon
August 2012

Carbon Copy Cowboy by Arlene James
September 2012

Look-Alike Lawman by Glynna Kaye
October 2012

The Soldier's Newfound Family
by Kathryn Springer
November 2012

Reunited for the Holidays
by Jillian Hart
December 2012

*Available wherever
books are sold.*

www.LoveInspiredBooks.com

LICONT0912